The French Kiss

The French Kiss

A novel by PETER ISRAEL

THOMAS Y. CROWELL COMPANY
New York   Established 1834

Designed by Ingrid Beckman

Manufactured in the United States of America

Library of Congress Cataloging in Publication Data

Israel, Peter, fl. 1967-
    The French kiss.

        I. Title.
PZ4.I84Fr   [PS3559.S74]   813'.5'4   76-6549
    ISBN 0-690-01099-0

1   2   3   4   5   6   7   8   9   10

The French Kiss

ONE

THE ADDRESS WAS for a hôtel particulier in a side street off Avenue Foch in the 16th—a section of Paris us commoners don't often get to see from the inside. If you don't have a *de* in front of your name, you pretty much have to be a cabinet minister or a call girl to live there, and when you got into that particular courtyard, you could all but hear the rattle of the coach-and-fours on the cobbles and the fanfares of the trumpets. As it turned out, one of Napoleon's generals had built it for his mistress, and to judge, he must have been running the blanket concession during the retreat from Moscow.

I came puddle-jumping out of the dark and rain and went under the porte-cochère on foot behind a swishing Bentley. In front of the glass-canopied entrance on the far side of the courtyard, a chauffeur was helping a couple in evening dress out of a 604 while the Bentley waited its turn. A pair of black brothers stood by in

black suits, holding umbrellas instead of spears, while
a third checked pedigrees and invitations. I handed
him mine, thinking they sure were growing them big
down on the Ivory Coast, and followed the couple in,
footman-style, past a gold plaque that said simply:
ALAN DOVE, *courtier en tableaux.*

I went up a flight of polished marble stairs. Even
before I reached the top, I could hear the clink and
babble of the *tout-Paree*, and there was enough fur in
the cloakroom to populate half the zoos of Europe.
The *tout-Paree?* Well literally it means "all Paris," but
from the point of view of the *tout-Paree*, it's "all Paris
minus the slobs." The *tout-Paree* is everybody who's
somebody plus everybody who wants to be, and it runs
from starlets to promoters, from novelists hustling
prizes to politicians peddling influence, from cou-
turiers and fleshmongers to chic freaks and fashion-
able hoods, and the whole held together by a sort of
free-floating cement of bearded revolutionaries and
fading beauties from the upper Paris bourgeoisie.
Conversation is their stock-in-trade, meaning mostly
that they make a lot of noise, all in that high-pitched
Parisian twitter, and they've got the swarming instinct
of bees. It doesn't take much to bring them out either,
just Culture with a capital C, plus a few caravans of
canapés and enough champagne to overflow the
Seine. In a pinch, the bubbly would probably do.

This wet spring night, though, it was Art that had
congregated them. Art with a capital A. A for American. Or A, maybe, for Alan.

M. Alan Dove, the engraved card had said, *invites his
friends to view some of his latest acquisitions.*

And to think I'd known him when his name was Dovici.

I stood at the fringe, watching the banks of smoke curling over their heads to flatten against the Napoleonic ceilings. Already they were jammed between laden buffet tables: short and bulky men in tuxes, sharp-featured dames sipping champagne in St. Laurent pantsuits, and the inevitable operetta of liveried young queens off the rack at Pierre Cardin, with the elevated shoes and the upswept shoulders. Somewhere behind the din a rock group was playing, and I was pretending like I was looking for someone I knew when a piece of the décor broke off from a wall and headed my way.

She was tall and tawny-blonde, and aswirl in chiffon, and she hit me with a gust of perfume, followed by a smile so wide you could see the magnolias blossoming in it, and the darkies swaying in the cotton-fields.

"It's so nice of you to come!" she said in a breathy Southern warble. "My name's Susan Smith, I'm from Savannah, that's in Geo . . ." She broke it off and laughed, tossing the tawny-blonde. "But you're American too, isn't that raaa-ht?"

"That's right," I said. "Cage is the name. I'm from Yakima, that's in . . ."

"Yakima, Washington!" she exclaimed. "But what a wonderful *surprise*! I never met anybody from *there*!" Then, hooking her arm through mine: "But aren't you interested in seeing the paintings? Wouldn't you like me to show you aroun'?"

"I'd like that just fine, Susan Smith," I said. "But tell

me, what's a lovely young thing from Savannah, Georgia, doing in Paris, France?"

Chuckling throatily, she steered me into a hole in the mob.

"You're a funny man, Mr. Cage. But there are just *loads* of Americans in Paris, didn't you know?"

"I guess I did. But do you work here?"

"I sure do!" she shouted at me. "I majored in art history, with a minor in French!"

"You mean you work for Al Dove?" I shouted back.

"I sure do! Isn't it exciting?"

I wasn't sure whether she meant Paris or working for Al Dove or majors in art history and minors in French, but right then there was no finding out. The *tout-Paree* engulfed us. It seethed and smashed like surf, and every time you came up for air, the Art pounded you back down again. It was everywhere you turned, and so loud you could hear the neon shrieking on the Vegas Strip, smell the Monroe brand of sex oozing off the celluloid. Though I'd have been the last to judge what it might have been worth in dollars or aesthetics, it was big and gaudy and ultra-American, and it sure had stimulated the *tout-Paree* right out of its cosmopolitan socks. The electric-guitar background must have helped too, also the décor—call it one-third Napoleonic and two-thirds acid modern—also the other larger-than-life Susan Smiths I saw circulating in the crowd, with those wide-mouthed, help-yourself American smiles. But you could hear it in their decibels, feel it in their heat: a fever of excitement such as Parisians usually reserve for itinerant sopranos and conquering generals, and if it didn't particularly infect me, it must have been because I hadn't been away from home long enough to feel the full impact of a promotion made-in-U.S.A., snake-oil division. Then too, I may as well admit right now that my taste in modern art pretty much began and ended with the work of R. Crumb.

Somebody had stuck a champagne coupe in my hand. I hung onto it, and Susan Smith, and together we fought our way through a series of jammed reception rooms. As we went, she laid it all on me breathlessly, not only who'd painted what, but when, and what they'd had for breakfast that morning, and she sprinkled in bunches of names—deKooning, Kline, Blumenstock—that sounded like double-play combinations off the old San Francisco Seals. The main event, it seemed, was going to be the unveiling of a Blumenstock. And not just any old Blumenstock either, but a late one, never before shown in Europe and rarely seen anywhere. According to Susan Smith, it was a masterpiece and Al Dove had more from the same period. But if, as we went, I spotted the man who'd paid me to come that night, our host was nowhere in sight.

"Isn't it *wonderful!*" she exclaimed when we came out at the other end. Her eyes were all aglitter and little beads of sweat had broken out in a pretty tiara across her forehead.

"Sure 'nough," I said, while I counted my limbs. "But what about the man who's responsible for it? Doesn't he come to his own parties?"

"Who, Al? Why of course! He'll be down for the Blumenstock!"

"*Down?*"

"Oh you know Al, he's always got to do things
. . . well, *theatrically*, don't you know? He'll stay
upstairs till the last minute, pretending he's got work
to do." Upstairs, it turned out, were offices and Al
Dove's private apartment. "But you *do* know Al, don't
you, Mr. Cage? Isn't that what you said?"

"No I didn't. But I do. How'd you guess?"

It flustered her momentarily.

"Oh I don't know," she said, "I guess I just thought
. . ." Then, smiling mischievously: "Well for one thing,
you don't honestly seem *that* all interested in the paintings. For another, you don't seem to know anybody
else here, present company excepted, and you just
don't strike me like the kind of man who'd come to a
party just for the champagne."

"You'd make a pretty good detective, Susan Smith,"
I told her. "But actually I haven't seen your boss in
four, going on five, years."

"Four *years*? But that must have been back in
California!"

"So it was. He wasn't in the art business either."

"But he knows you're here, doesn't he?"

I shook my head. "Not that I know of."

"He *doesn't*? Well why didn't you say so, silly? Let's go
find him!"

"I don't think we'll have to," I answered, looking
past her pretty head. "That's the great man himself,
isn't it?"

It came out casually enough, but I'd be lying if I
didn't confess to a certain inner twinge. He was a

couple of salons off, and headed in our direction. He had on a cream-colored, safari-cut nubby silk suit, the jacket unbuttoned, a darker silk shirt with long and open collar points and a foulard knotted Western-style around his neck, plus assorted jewels and chains, but except for the threads he hadn't changed: the dark hair, the dark-olive skin, the dark eyes set close to the nose, the same fine features except for lips on the full side. Maybe to you and me he wouldn't have made that much of an impression—after all, you can make Al Doves by the dozen, tooling around Malibu or Century City or Beverly Hills in their silver shades and rented Porsches, and I'd had the added disadvantage of having known him in chinos, not to say fatigues—but to the Paris crowd, in that setting, he was the genuine exotic article. You could see it in the way they stirred and shifted, the numbers arching their necks and jockeying to get their good profiles into his line of sight, and when they made way for him, all you could think of was the Red Sea the day Moses made his move.

"Isn't he *wonderful?*" breathed Susan Smith beside me.

"Yeah," I said. "Wonderful."

His eyes picked up mine when he was about a room away. He didn't recognize me at first and then he did, and we had a split-second's High Noon over the heads of the *tout-Paree*. *It's just a coincidence, Al,* I told him with my eyes. *Sure, Cagey,* he answered, *whatever you say,* and then he grinned, yelled something, and flung his arms wide, and the crowd did its Red Sea bit.

We met in a clumsy embrace. I held out my hand but

he went inside it into a sort of cross between the French
double-cheek smooch and the Mediterranean back-
thump.

"*Mon très cher ami*," said Al Dove.

There was the licorice laugh I'd forgotten about,
and the way his voice had of dropping in pitch and
volume when he got excited, all the way down to a
whisper when he was really turning it on.

"Geezus, Cagey," he said low, "it really is you, isn't
it?"

"None other, Al."

"After all this time! And no hard feelings, right
babe? But what the hell are you doing in Paris? Isn't it
the greatest? *C'est fabuleux, mon vieux!* I want to hear all
about it. Hey, have you met everybody? Hey baby"
—this to Susan Smith—"have you been taking good
care of my ole buddy here? Introducing him and
everything?" Then turning: "*Hélène, viens que je te
présente à mon ami Cagey*," then louder, waving his arm
for silence, his other arm slung around my shoulders:
"*Mes chers amis . . .*"

It was vintage Al Dove, all of it, with the French
thrown in.

There was a woman standing behind him. I'd never
seen her before, though I'd been told to look out for
her. I heard him introduce her later as "America's
foremost art critic," but from her get-up you'd have
thought even the art world had its poverty corner. She
was dumpy and medium height, but her shape and
clothes made her look shorter. Her hair was black and
chopped, her skin bad, her expression sullen, and the
suit she wore was too big in the jacket, too long in the

skirt. We shook hands, but Helen Raven's heart wasn't in it; neither, I guess, was mine, and whatever words we exchanged are distinctly unmemorable.

Because then it was a case of Cagey-meet-Paris, or Paris-meet-Cagey. It was hail-hail-the-gang's-all-here, with one arm around Helen Raven and the other around yours truly, and we were all "ole buddies" or "*très chers amis*," including ironically my most recent client to whom I was introduced along the way, and if Al Dove really wondered what his ole buddy Cage was doing in Paris or why he'd showed up this particular night, he made up his own answers and drew his own conclusions. Because he was too busy, as it were, taking his ole buddy Cage up the mountain and showing him the view, or that part of the view that was visible and meant to be seen: the success and glory of Al Dove Enterprises, Art Division, and if the guided tour came out half in French and half in English this time, it made no difference. Because I'd been there before, and often enough to have known without briefing that the art operation would have another seamier face, way down below where the deals were made and money went from hand to hand.

Like I've said, the name of the game this particular night was Blumenstock. It was in the air, Blumenstock, and the *tout-Paree* was already plugged in. A few years back, the painter in question had tried to dive off a bridge somewhere in New England, and maybe he'd've made it if he hadn't been behind the wheel of a car at the time. He'd been fried to the eyeballs, a condition presumably of several years' duration, and the scandal sheets had gone to town on dope, booze, and the tragedy of Great American Artists generally. There'd been something more, some kind of court battle, and then he'd been sent on to painters' heaven. But what I didn't know till later was that . . .

Well, but there were a lot of things I didn't know till later.

It was hanging behind floor-to-ceiling velvet draperies on a huge wall in the central salon. Several lengths of velvet rope cordoned it off from the mob. As we worked our way toward it, the rock group stopped playing and the lights dimmed. A cluster of spots went on in the ceiling overhead, and a minute later the din had ebbed so that you could hear the clink of glass in the background.

"Now you're going to see something, Cagey," Al Dove whispered to me.

He stepped over the velvet rope and onto a small platform. The spots framed the upper part of his body. He surveyed the *tout-Paree* and I could feel them pushing forward at my back.

"*Mesdames, Mesdemoiselles, Messieurs,*" he began, "*mes très chers amis . . .*"

He went into a short speech, punctuated by an occasional exploding flashbulb and delivered in a glib and smoothly accented French. John Blumenstock, he said, had been a great American painter. His work, universally acknowledged, was on display in museums and collections around the world. But what were largely unknown, and seldom seen, were the great canvases of his last years. It was an honor, said Al Dove, for him to have been able to acquire several of them, and a privilege, said Al Dove, to show one of them for the first time to the public, here in Paris, among his *très chers amis.* But what was he, asked Al Dove, but a humble dealer in works of art? Therefore he had invited the distinguished art critic, Professor Helen Raven, to come to Paris and join him in presenting this remarkable late work. For if many people knew Helen Raven as a critic and mentor, and others as having been a close friend of the artist, few realized the depth of her personal sacrifice in behalf of this great art.

"*Je vous présente ainsi . . .*" said Al Dove. There was a smattering of applause, and Helen Raven stood next to him under the spots.

An unlikely couple, I thought, while one of the Susan Smiths handed them up the drawstrings to the drapery. I felt the push again behind me, the heat of bodies in semidarkness, followed by a great communal "Ahhhhh" like a sigh, and louder applause, and exclamations of "*Bravo!*" and "*Magnifique!*" when the velvet curtains slid aside.

A man and a woman were sitting side by side on a couch in a living room. An enormous hound was stretched out on the carpet at their feet. The couch too was larger-than-life, a big overstuffed job in a garish luminous purple, and either it or some other trick of perspective diminished the couple. Their feet were hidden by the dog, but you got the impression they didn't reach the floor. The man had a ravaged face that was twisted into a half-smile or a half-grimace, you couldn't tell which. Somehow I got the idea he was John Blumenstock. He wore a maroon smoking jacket, and the woman, a lime-colored dressing gown with ruffles on the shoulders and a turban around her head. She was sitting straight up, which made her taller than the man, and staring straight out in a kind of stiff-necked, somebody-just-goosed-me expression.

They weren't very nice-looking people, whoever they were. They also looked, and everything around them, like they'd been painted within an inch of their lives.

Then a lot of things happened at once. All of a sudden there was renewed pressure at my back, like somebody had fainted or dropped a stinkbomb in the middle of the crowd. I heard shouts behind me, indignant. First one, then echoes of it all around. Catcalls and whistles, like what the bull gets when he refuses to charge. And though it took me a minute to understand and translate the message, then it came through, loud and raucous:

"C't'un faux! Scandale! C't'un faux!"

Faux, friend, is French for *fake*.

Helen Raven got the message too. I was watching her scarred sullen mask under the spotlights. I saw it frown, then stiffen in anger. Then a UFO whizzed over my head to crash in a tinkling of glass, followed by another larger one that exploded against the wall above the picture in a shower of bubbly. Then Helen Raven ducked and I heard, or saw, Al Dove shouting something—maybe *Wait a minute! Wait a minute!*—but who could hear him? Because Keerist, I thought, the fucking French! I mean: who else could get exercised enough to start a riot over a painting? Where else in the world could you get the natives away from their television sets long enough to fill a hall over a six-by-eight piece of canvas much less go to war over it?

Because that's what it was. It was 1789 and 1870 all
over again, and it erupted faster than you could shout
"Storm the Bastille!" One minute they were all puck-
ered and docile in their *tout-Paree* finery, the next a
surging shrieking mob. I mean people were actually
throwing things, like bottles and punches, and you can
say all you want about what happens when you pack
too many mortals into too small a space and booze
them up and turn down the lights, and theorize till
you're blue in the face about the madness of crowds.
Me, I still say: the fucking French.

But of course they had help. It had to have been.
Maybe one man with lungs enough could have pulled
it off, like a single spark combusting a forest fire, but
chances were he had a half-dozen or more accomplices
scattered in key places, with goblets in their hands and
flagons in easy reach and no particular compunction
about who they slugged or what with. Half a dozen
maybe, and then, with the crush and the semidarkness,
the *tout-Paree* did the rest. Undoubtedly they thought
it was a gag at first, an Al Dove happening, something
they could put down in their novels and memoirs, but
once the blood started to flow the joke stuck in their
throats and screams came out instead. People ran,
scattered, converged, fled. People had their clothes
ripped off. People fell and got stomped on. In a matter
of minutes it was a brawler's paradise, every man for
himself, women and children last, and it didn't simmer
down till the whistles started to blow.

As it happened, I was one of the first to go. A sudden
surge of bodies hit me from behind and the velvet
ropes tackled me neatly around the ankles. I went

down like a red-dogged quarterback and got up in a tangle, my hands trying to blot out the spotlights, in time to see a massive black fist thundering out of the ceiling like the hammer of Thor. Surprise, surprise, it was headed my way, but by the time I registered this unusual fact, all I could do was jerk my head back and take it on the shoulder. The jolt sent a shock of pain clear through to my big toes, and down I went again. This time I crawled around for a while on my hands and knees, cursing the referee, to surface in a gaggle of squawling pansies who were holding their nuts against all comers. A pair of arms was trying to grab me from behind. I ducked and pivoted and came up with my forearms extended, just like they teach you in Karate 3B, only to find myself wrestling with . . . my host.

"For Christ's sake!" Al Dove yelled at me.

He was quite a sight. Blood leaked from a corner of his mouth, and one sleeve of the silk jacket had been yanked half out of its socket. He was panting and heaving, and he had the desperate expression I'd seen before, of a high roller who won't admit the dice have gone cold.

"It's quite a shindig Al," I must have said, or some such.

"The bastards," he gasped at me. "I'll get them for this if it's the last thing I do!"

"Who's *them*?" I shouted.

"Listen Cagey!" A finger jabbed wildly at me. "It's gonna cost them triple now! *You* tell them that for me! *Triple!*"

"Who's *them*?" I shouted again, but there was no hearing his answer, if he had one. A new tide of bodies swept into us and crashed us apart. Somewhere in there the whistles started blowing and the lights went on again, but I wouldn't be too sure of the order of anything, only that when I glimpsed the *courtier en tableaux* again he was a salon away and heading out to sea. By this time I myself had been jammed backwards into one of the buffet tables. There was nowhere to go but up, so I watched the rest of the carnage, short-lived as it was, with one foot in a platter of sandwiches and the other in the caviar.

Short-lived, I should add, because of the arrival of the Law. I'll leave that part for you to put together. I mean, you've got a populace that on the one hand hires a police force big enough to colonize Mars and on the other shouts "Fascist pig!" every time they see a cop. I guess each of us has a little guilt tucked away in his soul, next to the stolen goods, but to see the *tout-Paree* cut and run that night when the Law showed up, you'd have thought the half of them had paintings stuck under their coats and the other half dope sewed in their linings. Well, but they don't do these things by halves in France. There must have been a couple of regiments of them, all in plainclothes and raincoats, including the ones who lined the staircase to make sure nobody ducked into the head. They didn't stop for any of the niceties either, like the customary identity checks. It was a case of *"Allez!"* and *"Dehors!"*, indiscriminately, which means *vamoose, beat it*, and as quickly as it had flared up, as quickly the party was over. Except for the stretcher cases.

Of these last there were relatively few—not so surprising at that in a country where hostilities are mostly

of the keep-me-away-from-him-I'll-kill-him variety.
The joint was a shambles, but the Art itself looked
largely unscathed. My client was long gone. So, it
appeared, were Al Dove and the Susan Smiths. In fact
the only familiar body I spotted was crouched in front
of the Blumenstock, her fangs bared and her claws
flying.

A gendarme below me said: "*Allez!*"

"*Dehors!*" said another to my right, and a third threw
in a "*C'est fini!*" for good measure.

Apparently they were talking to me. I've never been
particularly partial to the breed, but the odds for argu-
ment were all wrong, and if I needed any further
persuasion, it was the unceremonious image of Professor Helen Raven being separated from the Blumenstock across the way. At that I like to think the dame on
the purple couch snuck a peek just that once—it would
have pleased her no end—but as it was she continued
to stare out, haughty and stiff-necked under the turban. Straight out in fact at me. So I jumped down.

TWO

I CAUGHT UP WITH HER under the porte-cochère. The rain had settled into one of those steady silent mists that haloes the lights and soaks the pavement, and she was rubbernecking the street from the shelter of the arch, like Prince Charming was late with the chariot.

"Well, Professor," I said, coming up behind her, "you came a long way for a party, a shame it had to end so soon. But the night's young and Paris is all ours. And my humble droshky's right up the street."

I even gave her the bow that went with it.

Startled, she jerked her head at me. But then she registered who I was, and the anxious glance gave way to the same sullen expression I'd seen before. Without a word, she turned and headed up the sidewalk in the rain.

I kept pace with her. When we came level with the Giulia I stopped her.

"Here she is, Professor, four wheels and a motor."

Then, taking her by the arm: "Look, there's no point your getting soaked on a night like this. I'll drop you wherever you're going."

But some people are touchy, you could say. She whirled like I was a purse snatcher, and flailed, and slashed my arm away. Her eyes went big and nasty and froglike, and she brandished her fist in case I tried again.

"I don't know who you are or what your business is," she snapped at me. "But whatever it is, it's not mine. And I don't need your help, no thank you."

With that she pivoted and continued up the sidewalk. I watched her go in the dim light, nervous determined steps in an over-long skirt, but before she reached the corner I had the Giulia eased out of her slot by the curb. The street emptied out like the spoke of a wheel into one of those broad, cobbled Paris circles. The circle was deserted except for a couple of cabs waiting in a taxi rank on one of the far spokes. I saw Helen Raven run out into the slanting mist, waving her arm as she crossed, and by the time the cab made its U-turn to head down toward the Seine, the Giulia and I were right behind.

It was dumb enough in hindsight. The snooping expedition I'd been hired for, with Al Dove as primary target and Professor Helen Raven as a parenthesis, had obviously been derailed by the events of the party. Somebody had had a better idea of how to deal with my "ole buddy," and for the moment the most logical thing to do would have been to go home, nurse my aching shoulder over a bottle of Glenfiddich, and check in with my client in the morning. In addition, I was rusty as hell—enough, for instance, not to have noticed the absence of those unmarked blue buses they use to tote the Paris Law around in (by rights a dozen of them ought to have been parked in the circle), and the time had long since passed when I got my rocks off playing follow-that-car.

Maybe the rust had something to do with it at that, that itch you get from twiddling your thumbs too long while you're sitting on your hands and the Al Doves of your past are rolling high and rolling low. Also the memory of . . .

Well, but don't worry, it's all going to come out sooner or later. Chalk it up for the minute to my general conscientiousness, plus the fact that I never did take kindly to being rejected, not even by professors with scars on their cheeks and a pretty distinct aversion to the stronger sex in general.

We drove down the Right-Bank quays along the Seine, staying some two or three cars back in the flow. I expected the cab to peel off around the Concorde, where most of the posh hotels are, but instead he continued on into the tunnel, and out past the Louvre and the Cité, with Notre Dame looming up out of the mists, to veer off around the Hôtel de Ville. He went into the Marais, the old jewish quarter which has lately been rediscovered by the well-heeled ecumenical chic, but he wasn't stopping there either. He came out of it instead, through a maze of ancient streets, somewhere around the République. A couple of blocks later he trundled onto a short, arched bridge barely wide enough for a goat cart. It gave the distinct impression of crossing you into Transylvania. Down below was canal water, part of the old Paris locks system still in use, but which has to predate the wheel.

It made no sense, nor did the dingy street the taxi stopped in not far from the canal. The low façades had that warehouse look, but warehouses whose windows had been bashed in and whose brick walls were pasted over with tattered posters promoting French Algeria. One or two of the buildings were taller and might have qualified for residential, but they'd have been tenements in any other language, and all I could think of was that Al Dove sure didn't keep his guests in the style to which he was accustomed. Though in this, it turned out, I was wrong too.

I watched from the shadows while Helen Raven paid the taxi. She got out and fumbled in her purse in the doorway of one of the taller buildings. It was dark all the way up except, by sharp contrast, for light spilling out into the mist from a rooftop skylight. Maybe the Quasimodos lived there, I thought, and the bells would start ringing when I tried to follow Esmerelda through the door, but there were no bells when I crossed over behind her, and no buzzer either, none at least that you could operate without a key. I'd never seen the system before, but apparently it's used in over-the-hill neighborhoods no self-respecting concierge will live in. The front door's left open by day, but at night you need a key to trigger the buzzer, to get out as well as in, and if you've lost it, well, I guess they figure you can always make a rope ladder out of your sheets.

I stood there in the rain, contemplating the problem. Suffice it to say that I didn't hear him coming. All

I can tell you is that one minute my Adam's apple was
standing tall and that the next it was crushed into my
trachea by a forearm of steel. Then I was flung forward and crashed into the door.

The door hurt. So did my throat.

When I turned around, I saw the bulge in his raincoat pocket. He was black and big, bigger than big, and
if he wasn't the one who'd thorred me at the party,
then Thor had a twin spade brother.

"You're out of your mind!" I protested, once I'd
found my voice. "The Professor asked me over for a
nightcap, I was just trying to figure out how to get in
the damn door!"

This stopped him momentarily. He puzzled it over.
I tried it on him in French and was just about to switch
into Senegalese when he said:

"O.K., Mister Man, let's you 'n me go find out."

The accent, to my surprise, was pure Watts.

He had a key of his own. The buzzer buzzed and he
pushed me inside, into a dim and foul-smelling hall.
He shook me down. Then we went up a tunnel of
narrow wooden stairs where your head bumped the
light bulbs on the turns. The steps were scooped out
from use and slats were missing entirely in places, but
he didn't fall through. Nor did anyone come out on the
landings to see who was doing all the clumping.

The top landing had only one door. He knocked,
and almost immediately Helen Raven opened it. When
she saw me, she stopped whatever she'd started to say
and her expression went from surprise to anger. Then
a shove from behind propelled me past her and smack
into the middle of an artist's studio, one that looked

like it had been transplanted, paintbrush by paintbrush, out of the pages of *Vogue*.

It went up over two stories to an enormous slanting skylight. The front part was brilliantly lit, while softer lighting cast a glow over the living area, a double-decker affair in the rear topped off by a sleeping loggia. Above the loggia, from the peak of the slant, an elaborate system of spots shone down on a pair of tall wood easels, framed in the light like on the stage of a theater. It was *Vogue* all right, right in the middle of the Paris slums, and so was the vertical painter who stared at me from the easels, as un-Quasimodo as they come, a tall and spindly blond geek in a jeans outfit, with pale eyes, a high narrow forehead and wielding what looked more like a meat cleaver than a paintbrush.

"Evening," I said to him, holding out my hand. "My name's Cage."

"William Rillington," he answered, putting down the cleaver and wiping his long hands on a rag. But that was as far as it went, and virtually the last substantive thing he got to say.

"Shut up!" commanded Helen Raven behind me. The painter blinked rapidly at her. Then, to the spade: "Who told you to bring him here?"

"Who tole me?" he said. "Who tole *me*?" His voice went up in pitch. "Nobody *tole* me! I found the cat downstairs, Miz Raven."

"How'd he get there?"

"Looks like he followed you. He . . ."

"And so you had to bring him up?"

"He said you *ast* him over. That's what the cat said."

"And you believed him, didn't you?"

"I . . ."

But then he shut up too, and the rims of his eyes went sad and red like a spaniel's.

"You damn fool," she hissed at him. Then she turned to me.

"It's not his fault, Professor," I told her. "I just wanted to make sure you got home all right." I grinned at her, but it didn't make any dent in her expression. "Look, seriously, I'm sorry I barged in on you. Like your strongboy here says, it wasn't my idea, but nobody likes to stick around when he's not wanted. Obviously you've got better things to do. And so, I just remembered, do I. So why don't we call it a night?"

It sounded reasonable enough to me. With a wave, I nodded to them and made for the door, which was hidden somewhere behind the spade's bulk. He didn't budge though, except to bring the cannon out of his raincoat pocket. I couldn't see what he needed it for. It lay in his paw like a water pistol, with the squirt end pointed my way.

"Sit down," said Helen Raven.

"Lissen Miz Raven," interrupted the spade. "I can take care of the cat. Lemme take care of him for you. Lemme take him outside."

"Sit down, Mister Cage," she repeated.

Well, at least she remembered my name.

I sat. William Rillington sat. The spade sat, holding his cannon. And Helen Raven sat, but not for very long. She got up again, paced, sat down again. Then up again for variety, and so on. In between she chewed at her nails and stared at the telephone. But the telephone didn't ring, and nobody knocked, and every attempt I made at small talk came out mostly with me listening to my own voice.

I tried explaining it to the painter. It was all a mistake, I said. I was an old friend of Al Dove's. I'd gone to his party, there'd been a ruckus, everything had ended upside down. But I didn't know a Blumenstock from a . . .

"Where's Al?" Rillington wanted to know.

"Never mind," snapped Helen Raven.

"But he's coming over, isn't he?" the painter went on. "Or wouldn't he call?"

Silence.

"Maybe the police would know," I suggested.

"The pol . . ."

"*Never mind!*" Helen Raven shouted at him, on her feet. "*He'll get here when he gets here!*"

His reaction to this was to blink like a semaphore and shrivel in on himself, like his body was going to turn into a pipe cleaner. But seeing him, Helen Raven relented curiously. She murmured something I couldn't hear, the menace gone from her voice. Then Rillington unraveled, and she sat down again, and we listened to the rain against the skylight, which made no noise.

It was passing weird. The work-in-progress on one of the easels was Rillington's, I gathered. The other easel was bare. At least I took it for work-in-progress: with that kind of work I don't know how you tell when it's done. I think it's called "action painting," meaning, the way I understand it, that the painter hits the canvas with everything handy, including the contents of the garbage pail, and whatever sticks on, from noodles to gravy, is Art. It looked like a one-way grudge fight to me, and to judge by what I could see on his work table, Rillington had been using knives, hammers and broken bottles on the enemy. As to the result? Well, there'd been several such hanging at Al Dove's which Susan Smith had oohed and aahed over and they'd seemed no better or worse. Except that they'd been hanging at Al Dove's while Rillington's was still bleeding on the easel.

But for the area immediately around the easels, the place hardly seemed lived in. There was a complete kitchen unit under the loggia that looked right out of a box, and so did the furniture. Elsewhere, as far as I could see, the studio was bone bare. A series of walk-in cupboards ran all across one long wall. They looked far too big for clothes. The sliding doors were shut, there were locks on them, and I'd a hunch the Professor wore the keys chained to her navel.

Passing weird. A man called Bernard Lascault had hired me to do a little exploratory work on Al Dove, with a parenthesis on Helen Raven. He was a very persuasive character, Bernard Lascault; so was his checkbook. I'd gone to the party in order to establish contact, somebody had hollered "Fake!" and that had been the signal for the fastest scramble Paris had seen since they let loose a carton of mice at Pompidou's funeral. Then I'd ended up in a studio fit for Rembrandt, where I obviously wasn't supposed to be, in a neighborhood long since ready for the wrecker's ball, with a scarecrow of a painter, a bodyguard straight out of *King Kong*, and a professor who'd clearly spent too much time away from the classroom. Passing . . .

The phone rang.

Helen Raven had the receiver in her hand before the first ring ended. It was Al Dove, the courtier himself. Or—just maybe—the ex-courtier, to judge from the look on her face when she asked him about the painting.

Apparently she didn't like what she heard. There was a long pause. Then she said: "I see . . . yes, that's right, we'll make them pay for it." And then she looked at me.

She told him I was there. Apparently this created a considerable problem. There was another longer pause, punctuated only by her yeses and nos. Yes she'd been stupid, Helen Raven agreed, while she stared at me in that same sullen expressionless way that went along with her face, like the scars. Then finally, level-eyed and extending the receiver toward me:

"He wants to talk to you."

I stood up. Suddenly I felt tired beyond the hour. I was going back a ways mentally, in space and time, to the guy in fatigues and grinning under his crewcut, and back beyond that and forward to a lot of flickering images I'd long since stopped looking at.

"Is that you, Cagey?" his voice said.

"That's right, Al. And it's late and I'm tired. I think it's time you told your friends to stop fucking with me."

"*Me* tell *my* friends!" He laughed into the phone. That familiar licorice sound. "If anybody should be doing that, it's you, baby. Only I think it's a little late in the day."

"You've got it wrong, Al. Whoever's trying to stick it into you, I've got no part in it." Which was pretty close to the truth. "And anyway I don't see what I could do that'd hurt you now."

"You don't?"

"No, I don't."

"Like if I let you go, how long would you keep your mouth shut? Would you give me twenty-four hours? Cross your heart and hope to die?"

"Keep my mouth shut about what, Al?"

"Keep your mouth shut about what," he repeated. "Tell me, how much will twenty-four hours cost me? That's right in your line, Cagey, name your price. You've got a going rate, don't you? Hey, how about Binty? Remember Binty? Suppose I threw Binty in, would you give me a discount? Just for old time's sake?"

There was more to it than that, but I let him run it into the ground without answering. Somewhere along the way he started to laugh again. Maybe it was nerves, high-roller's nerves. Or something else. But what he was saying left me in no mood for analysis.

"Are you still there, Cagey?" His voice low.

"Yeah, I'm still here."

"You never do forget, do you." This needed no answer either. "Well, only this time, ole buddy, you're the one who's in deep."

"It doesn't look like I'm alone, Al."

"That's right," almost in a whisper, "and too bad I don't have you to help me this time. But I'm not in over my head yet. And you are. You are, Cagey. You chose the wrong side. If I was in my right mind, it'd be finished for you, ole buddy, all she wrote. But I owe you one. I don't forget either, baby. I'm going to pay you back, and then we'll be quits."

I started to say something, but the line had gone dead. I guess that was the signal they'd worked out.

I saw the brother stand, the cannon reversed in his paw.

Rillington and Helen Raven were standing too.

At times like that, friend, you've got two choices. Either you take it like a lamb, Auschwitz-style, or you give it the old college try. It's mostly a question of style, because either way the end result's the same.

I swung away from the phone and dove for him, driving low for his legs. I got there too, all the way in. Not that it mattered. Because meanwhile Black Thor had come thundering out of the spotlit heavens again, and there was a terrific crashing, like the old Kenton brass giving it the Grand Finale inside my skull. My muscles turned the consistency of doughnuts, and when he shrugged his knees I slipped off the deep end, out past the stars and the crashing, to where there's no music at all.

THREE

LET'S LEAVE THE BODY lay there. It won't wake up for a while, not even in what must have been a pretty considerable commotion.

I guess it stood to reason. Like when people asked me what I was doing in Paris, I used to say: "Call it a cross between early retirement and extended amnesia."

Actually a pair of numbers from Air France had been responsible for it. Solange and Brigitte were their names, and it was they, a few centuries back, who'd introduced the *partouze* to my corner of Southern California, along with other French exports like goat cheese and Cahors wine and, on special occasions, some of the best dope Marseille had to offer. The *partouze*, in case you don't know it, is a venerable French pastime. All it takes is cars and couples and a quiet place where x number of same can park undisturbed. It's like musical chairs, only nobody loses, and so popular in France that *partouzes* have been known to create traffic jams in the Bois de Boulogne at three in the morning. Anyway, we used to hold them out my way in Santa Monica, and then when the sun came up on the surf we'd run the girls back down the freeway to where the 747's dip in low out of the smog like big pregnant birds and off they'd go, half-stoned, into all that wild blue yonder us groundlings never saw, and leaving old homebody Cage to count his doubloons by the hearth.

Of the doubloons, I should say, there were sufficient at the time. My card says B. F. Cage, Public Relations, but the way I worked it, this meant mostly the gathering and suppression of information. Other people's dirty laundry in sum, and there was enough of it in Mansonland to keep a man of relatively simple tastes in Heinekens till the last of the 747's came home to roost. But then something came along which made further toil and sweat superfluous. It was very sweet and dirty and I've told the ins and outs of it elsewhere, but suffice it that I hit a bonanza, a bona fide Bell Fruit jackpot. With the result that when the girls ganged up on me on one of those crazy rides down to the airport, there was literally nothing to hold me back. Solange, I remember, was whispering sweet nothings about life in Paris while Brigitte kept her hand on the throttle even after I'd turned off the motor, and the movie on the flight was Elliott Gould in *The Long Goodby.*

I set up shop in the bridal suite of a small hotel off St. Germain-des-Prés, but as much of my time was spent in a picturesque little pad up near the Observatory in Montparnasse. Whenever Solange and Brigitte took off on the Tahiti run, Josiane and Sabine flew in from Anchorage with a suitcaseful of king crabs. The weeks turned into months, the months into centuries. The loving was mutual, sometimes communal, and I never looked back. For all I knew the biddy at my old answering service was still taking messages and the Mustang still tethered in the parking lot at L.A. International, racking up $5 a day for the concessionaires.

End of idyll, one slick wet night when I came back to the hotel to find a bulky florid-faced gent waiting for me in the bar. His name was Bernard Lascault, he had the afternoon *Le Monde* spread out in front of him, and he seemed impressed by the fact that he'd gone to so much trouble to seek me out. The name meant nothing to me, though the organization of which he was *Président-Directeur Général* did vaguely. It was called Arts Mondiaux. He pronounced organization with the British *eye*, and his accent was as impeccably Savile Row as his clothes, and when I told him I wasn't in the market to buy paintings, he laughed at the back of his nose the way they used to before the Empire went under. But his way of getting to the point was strictly Latin.

A half-hour and a couple of Glenfiddiches later, I was still waiting for him to get to it. In the meantime I'd been served up a pretty heavy lecture about the international art trade. The gist of it was that the market had been going up and down like a yo-yo. New money had come in, new sources had opened up, and the pros had lost control. The big curators and collectors of Europe and America had been pushed aside by total strangers, and I suppose it didn't help any that some of the total strangers paid in yen while others faced Mecca in the morning before they brushed their teeth. There were sudden trends and even suddener flops, and posturers and simpletons on both sides of the checkbook. As a result, some works of art were traded at unthinkable prices, but a lot more had been quietly withdrawn from sale. Some of the long-established galleries were even in serious financial difficulty.

"Don't misunderstand me, Mr. Cage," said Bernard Lascault, "none of this has yet to have a direct effect on my organ-eye-zation. In point of fact I believe that a certain shaking-out process would be a very beneficial, a healthy, a necessary thing. Besides Art—real Art, good Art—remains one of the soundest placements an astute investor can make, the more so in precarious times."

Well, glad as I might have been to hear it, I still didn't see what it had to do with me. And I was on the verge of saying so again when he changed the subject.

"Tell me if I may be so bold," he said, gesturing at my pipe, "what's that tobacco you're smoking? It has an unusual aroma, very pleasant."

"It's Erinmore," I answered. "Murray's Erinmore Flake."

"Odd name."

"It's Irish."

"Irish? You're not Irish in origin by any chance?"

"No," I said, "but I like their tobacco."

"And the Scottish, I notice, for their whiskey?"

I nodded.

"And us French . . . ? For our women?"

If this lit a small warning in my brain, I paid it no attention. He stared blandly across at me, between heavy lids that looked like they were standing guard over his eyes. Then he said:

"Tell me, Mr. Cage, what do you know about a certain Alain Dove?"

I did a double take over the way he pronounced the name, then a triple take and a lot of other takes besides. He was a lot cuter than I'd given him credit for.

"I used to know an *Al* Dove," I said, "if we're talking about the same person."

"I think we are," Bernard Lascault answered mildly.

"I haven't seen him in years. The last I heard of him he was up to his neck in a California real-estate mess. You could look it up, it made the headlines."

"Yes. It was called Rancho del Cielo, wasn't it?"

"That's right."

"And before that? There was some sort of obscure affair concerning drugs in which you yourself were somehow involved, if I'm not mistaken?"

"An obscure affair," I agreed. Maybe it was around in there that my palms began to sweat, just a little.

"There was a woman involved in it too, wasn't there? Who later became Mrs. Dove?"

"That's right."

"Yes. Well then, suppose I were to tell you your friend has since become . . . how shall I say? . . . one of the hottest dealers in the field of international art?"

I thought it over.

"Well," I said, "you yourself talked about posturers and simpletons . . ."

He laughed heartily at that, all the way down to his epiglottis.

"Posturer perhaps. But simpleton? I'd hardly think so."

According to Bernard Lascault, Al Dove was primarily a dealer's dealer. In French they called that a *courtier.* He'd hit the market like a thunderstorm a few years back, and the new American boom in Europe had been largely his doing. All the established galleries had dealt with him, Arts Mondiaux included, and if there'd been one or two "disquieting" incidents, nobody had asked too many questions. But conditions had changed, the market had gone soft, and Al Dove lacked control. At least that was how Bernard Lascault put it. The way I interpreted it, in a seller's market anything went, including your Great-Aunt Minnie's childhood etchings, but when the buyers started staying home, then people began to worry about finer points, like maybe stolen goods.

"His ambition, one might say," Bernard Lascault went on, "has got the better of him. Now were the problem limited to him, one might say: too bad and . . . what is it? . . . good riddance to bad rubbish? But of course it isn't. Mr. Dove's problem is ours. In point of fact, his lack of control is jeopardizing us all."

"Why don't you tell him so?" I asked.

"Ah, but we've tried. Of course we've tried."

"And?"

"We have an expression: *le vent en poupe,* how do you say it in English? *The wind in the . . . sails?* Sometimes it is very difficult to convince people who have the wind in the sails."

That sounded like Al Dove all right, the same one I'd known.

"And what about the Law?"

"Do you mean the police?" He grimaced at the idea. "No. Of course the police have their purposes, but that would be premature. Quite premature. Besides, I'm not sure it could be proven that Mr. Dove has done anything illegal, even if one wanted to."

"I see," I said. "And, to quote you another expression, you also don't want to kill the goose that lays the golden eggs."

"The goose . . . ? Oh yes, quite."

"And so you've come to me?" He nodded. "Well, flattering as that might be, Mr. Lascault, what makes you think I'd be able to convince him where you haven't? I mean, I suppose I could rough him up for you a little, but . . ."

He started to shake his head, then settled for that condescending nasal laugh.

"Ah, you Americans!" he said. "You always see life in such primary colors! But Paris isn't Chicago, Mr. Cage. The situation is rather more delicate. All we really want right now is information."

"What sort of information?"

He leaned forward heavily in his chair.

"Information as to his sources. Who is backing him. Where the works he offers really come from, what his financial relationships are. Of course some of this is known to us already, but not all. For example, we know that the greater part of his business is carried on with a

well-respected gallery in Beverly Hills, California, the
current president of which is . . . Alain Dove. If you
see what I mean."

I saw what he meant, only not as far as I should have.
After all, if Arts Mondiaux was, as he put it, such a
farflung organ-eye-zation, with branches in L.A. and
San Francisco among other places, then why . . . ? But
my mind must have been on other things. Like how it
isn't every day you get to look up an old buddy. And
get paid for the privilege.

"So you're suggesting what?" I asked. "That I look
him up, say just for old times' sakes? And start asking
questions? And that—just for old times' sakes—Al
Dove's going to let me in on his trade secrets?"

He shrugged, and smoothed his thinning hair with
his hand.

"Stranger things have happened," he said imper-
turbably. "Mr. Dove can be a very free-speaking person. We also understand that you are a very resourceful one."

"Who told you that, Mr. Lascault?"

"As I've said," he replied mildly, "we've quite good
sources. In California as well as Paris."

"And what else have they said about me?"

"That you're good at your work, tough and good.
Also that your past relationship to the man in question
has been, shall we say . . . equivocal? Also that once you
commit yourself, you're to be trusted . . . up to a
point."

It was nice to know that my reputation was still
intact.

"Up to a point?" I said.

By way of answer, he reached into his suit jacket and pulled out his checkbook.

The parenthesis about Helen Raven came later, by telephone, and the invitation to Al Dove's party by messenger. Who was Helen Raven? I wanted to know. An art critic, he said, of a certain minor reputation. Also a professor somewhere on the West Coast. But what interested him was the precise nature of her relationship with Al Dove.

Somebody ought to have warned me, though, about large men with small laughs. A clever operator, Monsieur Bernard Lascault. He had help from his checkbook too, but when you're handing out the gold stars, don't forget that across from him was a stud whose palms went sweaty, just a little, at the mention of certain names, and the memory of old, unsettled scores not all the stews and *partouzes* and other sweet diversions of Paris, France, had quite managed to bury.

Rusty, like I said.

FOUR

THE PAIN STARTED right behind my eyeballs. It stayed there pretty much as long as I didn't move, but I was being dragged up toward the light like a hooked fish, and the brighter it got, the more the pain scorched my nerves. The insides of my eyelids went from purple to orange to a searing white and the empty space between my ears started to smoke like dry ice. Somewhere near the light I wrenched and lurched, and there was a blinding, tearing sensation when the hook pulled loose, and after that I must have drifted off for a while, down toward the cool swooning depths where the ones that get away swap stories in their old age.

Until it started getting lighter again.

Somebody groaned. That was me. I was looking at sky. The sky was a bright and sickish gray, and only a thin, slanting shield separated me from it.

I blinked. It hurt to blink. Something moved between me and the light, then away again. That hurt too, and I tried to lift my head up to tell whoever it was to cut out the movement.

Instead I threw up.

Whoever it was leaned over me, registering the event like an ichthyologist in an aquarium. Around in there, in no particular sequence, I realized that I had no sensation below my elbows or my knees, that the rest of me was sweating and shivering at once, also that the thin shield was the slanting skylight of the studio, only a lot closer than the last time I'd seen it.

After a while the ichthyologist hunkered down near me. He was a little guy with a wizened turtle's head, and he wrinkled his nose in distaste like he'd never seen one like me before. We stared at each other. He started asking me questions in a flat, functional language. After a while I realized it was French.

He had small, impervious eyes. Patient eyes. He wanted to know how I'd gotten there. I wanted to tell him too, but the nausea kept getting in the way. It came and went in clammy gusts, hot and cold. Not only had I been thorred but trussed and shot full of puke and thrown up on the loggia for good measure. I was spread-eagled on a mattress and left to bake under the skylight and Bernard Lascault was telling me Paris wasn't Chicago and Al Dove was paying his debts.

The ichthyologist called out from the loggia railing. A pair of voices answered from below, and I heard heavy footsteps on the staircase. Then I was flipped over, the mattress with me, and a minute later I rolled free.

I got to my knees, tried to stand up and fell on my face. They had to help me down the spiral stairs and hold me over the kitchen sink while I threw up again. Then they emptied me onto a couch and we started playing 20 Questions.

They were cops all right, but there was something different about the ichthyologist, even though it took me a while to find out what. His name was Ravier and he was a commissaire, but it was pretty clear he didn't like the sight of blood any more than he liked my story. For that matter, I didn't much like his either. The Law, it seemed, had gotten an anonymous tip, complete with address. A couple of bloodhounds had been sent over to check it out. They'd found the studio wide open, and me. They'd called for help, and the help had called for help, until it got to Monsieur le Commissaire. Only somewhere on its way up the totem pole, the news had apparently taken a sharp horizontal turn.

I told Ravier I'd been to a party given by an old friend of mine, a fellow American called Alan Dove. Monsieur Dove dealt in art, I said. I gave his address. There'd been a disturbance at the party, the police had been called. Afterwards I'd come to the studio with a friend of Monsieur Dove's, whose name was Helen Raven. She'd invited me back for a drink. There'd been two other Americans there, a painter called Rillington and a black man whose name I didn't know. What was the relationship between these people? They were all friends of Monsieur Dove's. But beyond that? I didn't know. Did they live at the studio? I didn't know that either. And had we been drinking or taking drugs? No, I'd had a glass or two of champagne at the party, that was all. But hadn't I said the woman had

invited me there for a drink? Yes, but we never got that
far. Oh? Why was that? Because I got hit over the head
first. And who had hit me over the head? The black
man. But why would he have done a thing like that? I
had no idea, maybe he didn't like white people. Oh?
And what had happened then? I had no idea, between
getting hit over the head and waking up was a total
blank. Or what had happened to the other people? No,
not that either. Then would I take a good look at the
studio and see if anything was different or missing?

One of the bloodhounds had been taking notes in a
small crabbed hand. The motion made me sick to my
stomach again. I lifted my head. The Rillington was
still on the easel, the mess on the work table. The rest
of the place had that same unlived-in look. But then,
on the other hand . . .

I was staring into those huge walk-in cupboards that
lined one wall. They were deep all right, with vertical
built-in racks, but clean as a whistle except for some
sheets of paper on the floor. Again, that unused look.
But then it suddenly hit me that I was staring *into*
them, and that the night before the sliding doors had
been shut and locked.

I got up, wobbly. They were deep all right, but the
racks were empty. I noticed some kind of thermostatic
deal that could have been a temperature control. *Could
have been used to store paintings*, a smart-assed little voice
said inside me. Could have been, I answered. (King-
sized paintings. Rillingtons? Blumenstocks?) I heard
Ravier asking something behind me, but my stomach
was already scrambling, and I felt an upward rush of
dizzying heat, and the smart-assed voice opined: *Hav-*

ing a little trouble working the pedals, honh, Cagey babe?

At which the little trouble became a big trouble and down I went again.

It was getting to be a habit.

Weak as my story sounded at the studio, it played even less well at the Quai des Orfèvres. It wasn't my idea to go there. I mean, I'd already seen the gold-spiked gates of Paris justice from the outside, which was close enough for me. Besides, as far as anybody knew, no crime had been committed, had it? Other than the one perpetrated on yours truly? And yours truly was ready to be big about it and forget the charges.

Then they had to go and switch audiences on me. Monsieur le Commissaire Ravier, it turned out, belonged to something called the Service de la Répression des Fraudes Artistiques, which means the guys who tap you on the shoulder when you start carrying the Mona Lisa out of the Louvre. But the Monsieur le Commissaire who took over at the Quai des Orfèvres was Police Judiciaire, which means plain old garden-variety crime cop. His name was Dedini, and he'd been at it for twenty-eight years. He didn't seem very proud of it either. He had the belly that went along with the job, and bulldog jowls pinched by his shirt collar, and a pair of rimless specs stuck on a massive head, and a dusty desk squeezed between filing cabinets and metal closets, and every time he said he'd been at it for twenty-eight years, his tone added: I'm up to my ears in it, Monsieur, don't think you're any different.

Dedini didn't buy my story, not at all. I think it was

congenital with him. I gave him a little more than I'd
given Ravier. I said I thought I'd been thorred because
Al Dove had ordered it. I gave him the phone call too.
Al Dove, I said, had been plenty agitated over what
had happened to his party, and he'd gotten the idea I'd
had something to do with it. In this he was 100 percent
wrong, but I was ready to let bygones be bygones.

Dedini shrugged. He ran his finger around inside
his collar, looked at the tip of it, then picked up my
passport again in both hands. He riffled the pages,
stopped, read, riffled some more. He'd already done
this several times. As soon as I'd got there, they'd put in
a call to the foreigners' section at the Prefecture of
Police. And had come up empty-handed. This wasn't
surprising—files aren't normally kept on tourists—but
it made Dedini suspicious.

How long did I say I'd been in Paris? he wanted to
know.

Off and on for some months, I'd already said. I said
it again.

Didn't I know any foreigner who spent more than
three months in France had to register with the Prefecture and apply for a *carte de séjour?*

Yes I knew that.

Well?

But I hadn't spent more than three consecutive
months in France.

Where else had I been?

I'd been to Majorca. I'd also been in Italy.

Then where were the stamps in my passport?

The border officials had only looked at my passport.
They hadn't stamped it.

I hadn't been conducting any business in Paris, had I?

No, I hadn't.

What precisely was my business?

Public Relations.

Where did I practice this Public Relations?

In Santa Monica, California, U.S.A.

In California but not in Paris?

That was correct.

I knew, didn't I, that any foreigner who worked or did business in France had to possess a *carte de travail*?

Yes, I'd heard something of the sort.

Monsieur Dove was also from California, hadn't I said that?

In fact I didn't remember saying it, but yes, Monsieur Dove was also from California.

Monsieur Dove was doing business in Paris, wasn't he?

Yes.

What did I know about Monsieur Dove's business?

Very little. He dealt in works of art, apparently successfully. It wasn't my line.

Then I didn't work for Monsieur Dove?

No.

Or have any business dealings with him?

No.

I knew, didn't I, that any foreigner living in France who wasn't regularly employed had to prove an adequate source of income?

I'd heard something of the sort. I didn't believe it applied in my case though, because I wasn't legally living in France.

What, in any case, was my source of income?

I was living off my savings.

My savings?

Yes, my savings.

What was the source of these savings?

That, I said, was my business.

Were there any persons in Paris who could attest to these statements?

Well, they could check the hotel I stayed at. The people there could vouch for my coming and going, also that I paid my bills.

Besides the hotel?

No.

No? Did I mean to say that I'd been in Paris such a considerable time and knew no one?

No, of course I knew some people in Paris.

Well then?

Well then, I didn't want them being bothered by the police.

And so on and so forth, or *ainsi de suite* as the French would put it. I took it at the time for one part fishing expedition and one part stall, with more than a dash of that sadistic pleasure bureaucratic work brings out in people. But I took it less and less, and when a bloodhound brought in a plate of sandwiches that looked suspiciously like rejects from Air France's propellor days, I broke out in a sweat again. I had nothing against cooperating with the police, I said, but I'd answered all their questions, more than once. Now I had better things to do. No crime had been committed. If they needed me again, they knew where they could find me. Etc. etc., and I salted and peppered it with lawyers, ambassadors, and the Declaration of the Rights of Man.

Dedini dropped my passport on his desk. He ducked his head, scratched his neck, then bit into one of the sandwiches.

"Sit down, Monsieur," he said between mouthfuls. "There have been two infractions of the law that we know of."

He picked up a newspaper with his free hand, flipped it open, and tossed it across his desk at me. It was the first edition of one of the afternoon papers and Al Dove, I saw, had made the front page.

"Sit down, Monsieur," he repeated. "Read it."

I sat down.

Un vernissage pas comme les autres (an opening unlike the others) ran the headline, and under it they'd used two photos. One was of the Blumenstock, the other, fuzzy but recognizable, of the mêlée. The story under the painting referred to an old controversy over the artist's late work and an American court case famous in art circles. Was the scandal about to revive? the reporter asked. In any case, he concluded, there hadn't been such a furor in the tired world of Art since the Legros affair, to which this one might bear more than one unsuspected resemblance.

"Theft," said Commissaire Dedini, taking another sandwich. "The first infraction is theft."

I didn't get it.

"The painting is missing," he said, pointing. "It is presumed stolen."

I still didn't get it. Who would steal a fake? Besides, hadn't it still been hanging there when the police showed up?

Dedini's mouth was full of sandwich, but that didn't deter him.

"Read the other one," he said, gesturing at the newspaper.

The second story was about the party itself. It described the same ruckus I'd witnessed, but it claimed that the carnage that had taken place before the police arrived was nothing like what had happened after. In the process of their seizing the premises—for what motives nobody knew—innocent people had been roughed up and brutalized. This was just another example, by now familiar to Parisians, of violence compounded by official violence. All too typically the police had no comment, and the citizens of Paris could only ask again: Who did the police think they were protecting, and from whom?

"The scum," Dedini said when I'd finished reading. He pulled out a handkerchief and wiped his mouth. "Was that what you saw, Monsieur?"

"It's pretty exaggerated," I said.

"Did you see any examples of this so-called police violence?" He gestured again at the paper. "Of innocent people being brutalized by the so-called police?"

"Not really. But . . ."

"The scum," he repeated. This time I assumed he was referring to the press. He took off his glasses, blew on them, then wiped them on the handkerchief. His eyes looked naked and watery without them.

"But what about the painting?" I said. "I still don't
see . . ."

Putting the glasses back on, he leaned back heavily in
his chair.

"Suppose I were to tell you, Monsieur, that there
wasn't a contingent of police within two kilometers of
your friend's party last night?"

I mulled that one over. The more I mulled it, the less
I could suppress a smile. Because if someone had set
me up, which was what it was beginning to look like to
me, at least I had company.

Dedini, though, didn't see the humor in it. His eyes
went small behind the specs and his lips tight like a
prune.

"If they weren't the police," I said, "then who were
they?"

He didn't answer, though somehow I got the impression he knew. I thought back to the ones I'd seen.
They'd looked enough like Law to me, and they'd been
well organized. Maybe too well? In any case, I hadn't
been the only one who'd been fooled. There'd been
the *tout-Paree*, and the press too.

"We want to talk to your friend Dove," said Dedini.
"Where is he?"

He stared at me. I stared back.

"I don't know," I answered. "You've got the same
address I do."

He ran the fingers of both hands through the gray
stubble of his hair. He didn't say the word this time, but
you could see it in the disgusted look on his face.
"Scum," and I guess for Monsieur le Commissaire it
meant everybody, present company included.

Just then we were interrupted. There was a knock, then the door to Dedini's office opened and a tall, dapperly dressed figure looked in from the corridor. He glanced at me without recognition, then crooked his finger and called to Dedini in a clipped peremptory voice.

The commissaire's jaw tightened. He got up and his lumbering body disappeared into the corridor. I could hear several voices arguing at once, but all I heard Dedini say was "*Oui, Monsieur*" and "*Non, Monsieur*," and when he came back he looked like he'd been taken by the collar and shaken inside out.

Two bloodhounds were with him.

"Let's go," Dedini snapped at me. He stopped only to grab another sandwich off his desk. Chomping at it, he led the way.

It had started to rain again, that chill spring drizzle, and the sky was going dark ahead of time. I spotted the Giulia parked where I'd left her, but if I'd've had a notion, the shift in the odds would have put it from my mind. It had been three to one in Dedini's car. Now, on the canal bank, it was more like two dozen, give or take a few.

What was it I said: one part fishing expedition and one part stall? But all the time the stall, if that's what it was, had been going on at the Quai des Orfèvres, the fish had been lying at the bottom of the Canal St. Martin. The Law claimed they'd gotten another anonymous tip, but I still like to think it was one of those old anglers on the canal banks who'd gotten his first bite of the century out of those polluted waters and knew something had to be wrong.

By the time we got there that particular lock had been drained to knee depth and the fish hauled onto the dirt bank. They'd covered him with a blanket. Three men in high rubber boots stood guard over him along with Monsieur le Commissaire Ravier, his turtle head scrunched against the elements, while behind them a squadron of uniformed gendarmes kept the curious at bay and the quay traffic circulating around the police vehicles.

It was a big one too, and as black as Italian coffee. He hadn't been in the water long enough for the body to have mildewed, but the whole right side of his face had been staved in, starting with the eye. By a club, you'd say, or even an irate mastodon, though as it turned out a single bullet had done the damage, a big and crashing one fired at close range.

I had no trouble recognizing him. It was Thor all right, the same oversized brother who'd kingkonged me at the party, again at the studio. Sometime after that, while I bad-tripped up on the loggia, somebody had taken him out with a Paris-isn't-Chicago elephant gun and dumped him conveniently into the canal. He didn't look like he knew what had hit him either, lying there soggily in the drizzle, and while I shed no tears over him, I felt no particular gratitude toward his murderer.

"I suppose you never saw him before," said Dedini.

"I've seen him," I said. "I don't know his name, but he was the one who slugged me last night. Both times."

The commissaire was holding the blanket up in one hand. He let it drop.

"Who killed him, Monsieur?"

"I have no idea," I replied.

Somebody handed him a manila envelope. It contained the so-called last effects of the corpse. He pulled out a passport, examined it, handed it to me. It was a green American Eagle job, and though the ink had run and some of the pages were stuck together, you could still make out: Name: JONNISON DAVIS; Birthdate: August 1, 1947; Birthplace: CALIFORNIA, U.S.A.

California, U.S.A. I shook my head.

"It's a big country back there," I said, "and California's the biggest piece of it. No, I never heard of him before."

We went back to the Quai des Orfèvres. Monsieur le Commissaire Ravier wanted a crack at me, but homicide wasn't art fraud. Homicide was strictly Police Judiciaire. That meant that Monsieur le Commissaire Ravier could go fingerpaint. That meant back to the same dusty office with the single grime-streaked window giving onto the courtyard, and murder made Monsieur le Commissaire Dedini happy as the proverbial pig in sunshine, the more so because he had a live body to go with the dead one.

The French Law, you see, have a nasty little wrinkle going for them. It's called the *garde-à-vue.* What it means is that they can hold you for twenty-four hours for no reason at all, and the twenty-four can go to forty-eight in cases involving "national security," which, the way I understand it, can include stealing a loaf of bread. You get zero phone calls. They don't have to tell a soul, not even your mother, and if they've got to take you before an examining magistrate after the time limit, they can lock you up and throw away the key in the meantime. Furthermore, the examining magistrate doesn't even have to be convinced you've committed a crime. He can order you held as a witness, and if there's the slightest doubt about your skipping town, not all the legal talent in Paris can get you out. Preventive detention, it's called, and according to Dedini, examining magistrates were used to cooperating fully with the Police Judiciaire in regard to preventive detention.

"Now, Monsieur," said the commissaire, swinging his spectacles in a heavy hand and creaking his chair, "I want to hear your story again from the beginning."

We went through it all again. Through the grimy window I saw some lights go on in offices across the courtyard. Later on they went out again. The normal working Paris slobs were going home. But apparently Dedini wasn't a normal working Paris slob. Apparently I wasn't either. For just that once, much as I hate to admit it, I wouldn't have minded being one. My nausea had worn off, but in its place was a cold, sore, and empty feeling. I'd had enough, and more than enough of that expression that came into the commissaire's gaze. You could call it his scum look, but I'd seen it before on functionaries of all sorts. It's bitter and smug at the same time, and maybe wearing it is the only satisfaction people like that get in their work, but it was pretty clear in Dedini's case that scum included not only me but himself too probably, and Madame Dedini if there was one, and all the little Dedinis.

We reached the point in my story where Jonnie Davis sent me down for the long count.

"Then somebody trussed me," I said, "and dumped me on the loggia, and maybe they shot me full of puke for good measure."

"Who?"

"How do you expect me to know? Maybe Davis did it himself. Maybe Al Dove did it."

"Why?"

"I've been trying to figure that out all day. I think probably somebody doesn't like me. I think I was in the wrong place at the wrong time."

"And then what happened?"

"All right," I said, "let's try it your way. Then I untied myself; then I pulled a cannon out of my underwear and shot Davis in the eye; then I loaded him on my shoulder, carried him to the canal, and dumped him in; then I went to Al Dove's, where the phony police were playing gin rummy, and swiped the phony painting; then I went back to the studio and tied myself up again; in between I emptied out the closets and swallowed the cannon whole; then I went to sleep."

The rimless specs were back on his nose. He looked at me over the tops of them. It was in his eyes then, and the sag of his jowls, the droop of his shoulders, the tone of his voice. Loud and clear. Scum, meet scum.

I dropped the name of Bernard Lascault in his lap.

It wasn't that he jumped up and faced the Arc de Triomphe the minute he heard it. From all I could tell, the name meant nothing to him. He wrote it down on a pad of paper. He drew a circle around it. Who was Bernard Lascault? he wanted to know. I told him. And what was my connection to him? I told him that too. But the more I told him, the more the expression went out of his face. Finally he picked up the telephone, dialed an inner office number, and by the way he said it as well as the words, I could tell he was talking up the totem pole all right:

"Excuse me for interrupting you, Monsieur. I need to see you immediately."

He listened a moment, then hung up. He sighed, got up heavily from his desk, and without so much as a glance at me, lumbered out of the office.

He was gone quite a while. When he came back, his face was gray and his jaw set like a cinder block. He didn't look at me, and what he had to say was addressed, in two short sentences, to one of the bloodhounds:

"They're waiting for him. Get him out of my sight."

It was within the same complex of buildings, but you'd never see a street cop in those carpeted corridors or the offices with those spacious paneled ceilings and crystal chandeliers and the flunkies to hold the ashtrays of the powerful even as they stubbed out their Murads. Most of it was dark by then, but the bloodhound led me through a paneled anteroom, and I saw Commissaire Ravier, pale and impassive, waiting

just inside a pair of open doors. Behind him stood the
tall, dapperly dressed man who'd summoned Dedini
out of his office earlier in the day.

There was a third presence too, though I didn't
make him out at first. He sat in shadow behind a small
and ornate desk. We weren't introduced. I never saw
him again after that night, and it wasn't till I ran across
his picture in a magazine that I identified him. Suffice
it to say that the ministry he ran had nothing to do with
the Law.

I was ushered to a chair near the desk. The
bloodhound stayed outside. Ravier and the dapper
man remained standing, and it was the dapper man
who did the talking.

"We've been trying, Monsieur," he began, "to deter-
mine your exact role in an affair which has certain
rather delicate aspects. According to our first analysis,
it was thought that you were simply an innocent par-
ticipant. This analysis, it now appears, was false.
Would you review your role for us please?"

This I did, including Bernard Lascault. I was getting
pretty good at it.

"Then according to this latest version," he said when
I was done, "you were engaged by a third party to
investigate Dove's activities. Is this version now final
and complete?"

"Yes it is."

"I take it you're a . . . what do your compatriots call
it? . . . a *private eye*?"

"Not exactly," I said, but the distinction didn't seem
to interest him.

"Why didn't you tell us this in the first place?"

"I didn't consider it relevant to your investigation. I also felt a certain obligation to my client."

His eyebrows went up in a sort of shrug, then dropped back into place.

"The Police Judiciaire, Monsieur, consider you something of a fool. We on the other hand are inclined to credit you with a certain intelligence."

"That's very flattering," I said. "But who's *we*?"

"We? Why the police in general. Or if you prefer," with a glance at Ravier, "le Service de la Répression des Fraudes Artistiques in particular."

There was an imperceptible stirring in the shadows to my left. My questioner seemed to take it as a sign of impatience. At some point he'd picked up a cardboard folder, tied shut with a ribbon. He'd tapped it in his palm while he spoke. Now he dropped it back on the desk and squared it with his fingers.

"The dossier is closed, Monsieur," he said to me.

It came out very flat, neat, and that was all there was. A pause.

"You mean that was a dummy you found in the canal?" I asked. "And the stolen painting's been returned?"

He shrugged again with his eyebrows.

"The police will continue to investigate these matters in their own way. They need no longer concern you. You are free to go. As far as you are concerned, you went to the Dove reception, and when the turbulence broke out, you left and went home."

I was home all right, on familiar turf. Commonly known as the cover-up. Only it felt passing strange to be on the receiving end.

"And what happened after that?" I asked. "Suppose somebody asks me what I did all day?"

"We think you are resourceful enough to handle such an eventuality."

"But suppose I decide to tell the truth?"

He looked as though this hadn't occurred to him. One eyebrow went up all by itself. He held it there a moment. I admired his control. Then it dropped.

"Perhaps you are forgetting something, Monsieur. France is extremely . . . flexible as far as foreign guests are concerned. Despite a long tradition of hospitality, there have been moments in our history when undesirable foreigners have been given twenty-four hours to leave the country. I see no reason why this couldn't be arranged in your case."

"As an undesirable guest?"

"Yes."

"And you would arrange it yourself if need be?"

"Personally," he affirmed.

Neat, like I said. So neat that it irritated me. As it happened I liked Paris, liked it very much.

"I'd feel a certain obligation to consult my client first," I said.

He shook his head. "Of course I'm sure I don't need to explain . . ." he began.

But at this point the minister cut him off with a wave. He leaned forward impatiently out of the shadows, the light shining on his sharp Gallic features.

"You are referring to Bernard Lascault," he said, making a statement out of the question.

"That's right."

"Then I'll have you know I talked to him, just a few minutes ago."

I didn't say anything. He stared at me, his eyes black and quick. Then he added, in a definitive tone:

"Bernard Lascault has informed me categorically that he has never seen nor heard of you, nor engaged you to work for him in any capacity whatsoever."

FIVE

THE PARIS GALLERY of Arts Mondiaux, S.A., was in a homey vault in one of the arcades off the Faubourg St. Honoré. It was all glass and high ceilings and tony recessed lighting, and though you couldn't see a sign of security, you got the feeling that if you so much as blew your nose in front of one of the paintings it would set off an alarm in the Elysée down the street and bring the President of the Republic on the double. As it was, no sooner did I set foot inside than one of those high-shouldered, power-driven manikins came pirouetting out between the partitions.

"Monsieur?"

"I'd like to see something about *this* big by *this*," I said in my best French. "It has to be green and blue predominantly. It's to go with a rug."

This broke his stride momentarily.

"Would you just care to look around?" he recovered

in English. "If you have any questions, I'd be more than happy to answer them."

"Some other time," I said. "In fact I'd like to see Mr. Lascault."

"Mr. Lascault?" One eyebrow went up. Eyebrows must have been in that season. "Mr. *Bernard* Lascault?"

"That's right. Are there any others?"

The second eyebrow joined the first, followed by the shoulder pads. There seemed to be some connection, though you couldn't see the wires.

"I'm sorry. I'm afraid that would be quite imposs . . ."

"Look," I broke in. "Suppose I came in here with a certified check for a million dollars and said I was ready to buy, say, Blumenstocks, what would you do?"

The shoulder pads dropped, followed by the eyebrows, followed by that bored expression he must have used on tourists from Dallas.

"I'm afraid Bernard's not here. He's very seldom . . ."

"But this is Arts Mondiaux, isn't it?"

"I'm afraid we're only the gallery. The offices aren't here."

"Where are they?"

"It's in the Bottin."

"The Bottin?"

"The directory."

"I don't happen to be carrying one around."

"Then you could ask for directory assistance," he said, topping me.

I smiled at him, most winningly. I was from out of town, I said, and an old friend of Bernard's, and what with my ineffable charm, I wormed it out of him. He wrote out the address on a gallery card, and I even got my palm tickled in the bargain.

I'd had a long night's sleep, a long bath, and a longer trans-world conversation with an old soak called Freddy Schwartz, who, drunk or sober, is the best source of information I know west of the Rockies. After that I'd had breakfast in the hotel garden, and then I'd picked up the Giulia by the Canal St. Martin. The sun was out, so were the fishermen, and I was off to discover why someone who headed such a farflung organ-eye-zation had hired me to find out what Freddy Schwartz had dug up on the spot in a single afternoon. And then why he'd fired me before I'd had a chance to show him half my stuff.

Call it curiosity if you like. But I had some other things in mind too.

After I left the gallery I pointed the Giulia up the Champs Élysées and sat back and admired the view. It's something to admire too on a day like that: the façades sunning themselves in even gray lines, and the clouds chasing each other eastward across that wide and horizontal sky, and the Arc de Triomphe presiding over it all. Not that it's the Paris Hemingway saw. When you look up toward the Arc now from that angle, a trick of perspective makes the towers seem to be rising right behind it, and you get one of those weird shrinking-world sensations, like they'd dried up the ocean to save space and that's New York City just over there, folks, where Paris ends. Only once you get up to the Etoile, which has been renamed Place Charles de Gaulle, you've still a chunk of the city to cross, followed by Neuilly, followed by the river, all

on a broad straight avenue, which has been renamed Avenue Charles de Gaulle, and by this time
you're thinking: that's not New York over there, that's
Moon City, and that they could have fit Manhattan
in between the skyscrapers if they'd wanted to. Maybe
taken by themselves the new towers are only dime-a-
dozen modern, but the ensemble is worthy of the
mad old Caesar who thought it up, and I still haven't
figured out why they haven't changed that name
too.

As it is, it's called La Défense, and there are only two
troubles with it. One is that it's still not finished, the
other, that whoever laid it out forgot that mere
humanoids like you and me were going to use it. Following the signs, I ended up parking the Giulia in
some sixth sub-basement down below the sewer line
and picking my way through a couple of miles of
construction sites, all this without a miner's helmet.
The moles who were doing the digging didn't speak
any language known to mankind, and it was sheer luck
that I found the tower I was looking for. But then an
elevator zoomed me up like a Minuteman missile
shooting out of a silo, and in no time at all I was back in
the real world of soft carpets, Mantovani, and
pushbutton phones, and doing my million-dollar cer-
tified-check bit for a frosted blond robot seated behind
a kidney-shaped reception desk with nothing on it but
her fingernails.

Not that it worked any better on her. No, I didn't
have an appointment, but wouldn't she tell Monsieur
Lascault I was there? Monsieur Lascault wasn't in his
office. Was Monsieur Lascault simply having an early

lunch and would he be back later? Monsieur Lascault wasn't expected in at all. Then what about tomorrow? She didn't know about tomorrow. Then what about next week? month? year?

At each of these questions the frosted blond thought a minute, then tapped out a combination on her console and checked at the other end. I kept at it until the computer itself came out to see who was crossing all the wires.

The computer's name was Madame Ducrot, and she had steely gray hair. She was Bernard Lascault's private secretary. She even had an office with a window in it and a view of another tower, although I didn't get to see it right off. First we parleyed back and forth a while in the reception area, until I pulled his check out of my pocket, a little frayed around the edges but none the worse for wear.

It wasn't made out for a million dollars, much less certified, but Bernard Lascault had signed it and it was drawn on an Arts Mondiaux account.

"This is highly irregular," said Madame Ducrot.

"On the contrary, it looks very regular to me."

"But I know nothing about it."

"Even so," I said, "you ought to be able to claim it as a business expense."

"But you haven't deposited it. Why haven't you deposited it?"

"Well if I'd deposited it, I wouldn't be having the pleasure of chatting with you now, would I?"

This seemed to melt a terminal or two. She flustered and simpered and patted her hair and glanced at the blond receptionist, and she didn't recover till she was safely in her office, with her desk between us and the check and my card spread out in front of her.

"Now Monsieur Cage, what exactly is it you want?"

"I want to talk to your boss."

"I've already told you: that's impossible. He's not in."

"When will he be back?"

"I don't know. He left no instructions."

"I think you should call him then."

"Impossible. Quite impossible."

"Really?" It was my turn to try the eyebrow bit. I guess it was contagious, and to judge from La Ducrot's reaction, I wasn't half-bad at it for a beginner. "An executive secretary who doesn't know where her boss is? Come come, Madame."

"But why is it so imperative that you see him?" she persisted. "Isn't it something we could help you with?"

"Normally I'd be delighted by that. But you see, Bernard Lascault retained me to get some information for him. I gather he didn't see fit to tell you about it, but by his own admission, he went to some considerable trouble to hire me. Not to say expense."

"Are you a private investigator, Monsieur?"

"Something like that."

Involuntarily her hand started up toward her hair.

"Well why don't you just make a written report then? I'll be glad to bring it to his attention."

I shook my head. "It occurs to me he might not want it in writing," I said, leaning forward. "Lest it fall into the wrong hands."

"Oh?"

God knows what seamy area of Bernard Lascault's

life, public or private, she thought I'd been digging into. I didn't elucidate. I simply narrowed my eyes a little the way you're supposed to, and let her imagination do the rest.

She hesitated.

"I think you should call him, Madame," I said quietly. "Now. I'll take full responsibility for it."

By this time I had worked my way around to her side of the desk.

"It's not that . . ." she began nervously. But then, changing her mind, she took her receiver off the hook and quickly punched out a combination of her own.

"Please!" she said, holding her hand over the mouthpiece. "Please be seated!"

Even computers, it seems, have lurid imaginations. I retreated and sat down.

There was no answer at the first number she tried, and whoever answered the second time wasn't on for long. La Ducrot announced herself, and then another voice broke in, and it wasn't Bernard Lascault's either in pitch or decibels. I couldn't make out the words, but it was one of those voices that don't need the telephone system to be heard. I caught it across the desk—loud, shrill, and angry—and lest there be any doubt in my mind, the secretary's expression did the rest.

"Who was that?" I said once she'd hung up.

She kept her hand clasped to the receiver. The backs of her knuckles had turned white.

"Madame Lasc . . ." she started, then jerking her head furiously in my direction: "That's none of your business!"

"What's the trouble?" I asked mildly. "Things aren't so hot at home?"

Her lips tightened. She started to retort, but her emotions caught her before a word got out. Then suddenly her whole face seemed to disintegrate. She blubbered. She stared out at me through squinting eyes, knowing it wasn't a pretty sight but helpless to do anything about it.

I reached for a handkerchief, but waving me off with her head, she opened a desk drawer and pulled a handful of Kleenexes from a box. With one wad she blew her nose, hard, then wiped at her eyes with another.

The storm blew past.

"I'm sorry, Monsieur," she said. "I . . ." She hiccuped, then mastered her hiccups. "I can do nothing more for you. I have your card. If you'll give me your address and number, I'll tell Monsieur Lascault you were here."

She reached out, but you've got to get up pretty early in the morning to beat me to the draw. While her hand was still in mid-air, I had the check folded in mine and halfway into my pocket.

"Never mind," I told her, patting her knuckles. "He knows where to find me."

As it was, she'd given me something to go on. Not a lot maybe, but you learn to make do. And more, as it turned out, than I'd bargained for.

The principal actors in the situation had all gone to ground. Before picking up the Giulia that morning I'd made a run past the studio. The downstairs door had been wide open, but there wasn't a sign of life on any of the landings. The studio itself was locked. I got the door open with my trusty hairpin and walked in. The only thing missing from when I'd last seen it, as far as I could remember, was William Rillington's work-in-progress. The Law, I figured, had gone in for art collecting.

Now, after leaving Arts Mondiaux, I drove back into Paris and over to Al Dove's. A gendarme was standing duty downstairs under the glass canopy, a real one this time.

He unfolded from the wall as I approached and blocked the entrance. At the same time he touched two fingers to the bill of his kepi.

"Stand aside, my fine fellow," I said. "I've an appointment with Alan Dove."

"No one's allowed in, Monsieur."

"Not allowed in? What do you mean, 'no one's allowed in?' I've got an appointment."

"Monsieur Dove's not here, Monsieur."

"Not *here*?" I glanced impatiently at my watch. "Well? Where is he? This is absurd! I'll have you know I've got an appointment to see his collection!"

The gendarme shrugged, but he stood his ground. I tried to maneuver around him but his body cut down the angle. We bumped.

"No one's allowed in without special authorization, Monsieur."

"Special authorization? But this is an outrage! I don't need special authorization, my good man, don't you know who you're talking to?" He didn't seem to at that. "Well? Where do I have to go to get this special authorization?"

"To the police, Monsieur."

"The *police*? But you're the police, aren't you? Say, but nothing's happened to him, has it? What's happened to him? I demand to know what's happened to Alan Dove!"

"No one knows what's happened to him, Monsieur."

"No one *knows*? But that's an outrage! I demand to see the person in charge!"

I maneuvered again. We bumped again.

"I'm sorry, Monsieur," he said, nodding toward the sky. "There's no one up there who knows any more than I do."

"Who's up there?"

"Just some of my colleagues, Monsieur. And the paintings."

I could have tried the old BF Special on him, the fullback up the middle without the ball while I snuck around end for the winning touchdown, but I figured he'd bring up the cornerbacks if I did. Instead I went off, muttering "outrage" and "special authorization" till I was out of earshot, and when I took a last look back from the porte-cochère, he was slouched against the entrance again, staring at nothing.

So Al Dove had disappeared, it seemed, along with his team, and the Law had his collection, and from what Freddy Schwartz had told me plus what I'd picked up on my own, I had one or two pretty good theories as to why. But Bernard Lascault was lying low too, which didn't square either with the theories or with the Law having "closed" the dossier.

As it happened, I'd called Freddy Schwartz right after my first meeting with Lascault. Freddy's a sad and bleary-eyed old rummy who'd lost his job on the L.A. *Times* mostly because of the booze. But like I said, he's still a useful little guy, even though when he'd called me back that morning, it had been midnight in Los Angeles and to judge from the rolling sound of his voice he'd been well on his way to bottle heaven.

According to Freddy Schwartz, the gallery in Beverly Hills was a real go-go operation but strictly kosher. Al Dove was listed as president, but the person who ran the show on the spot was Mrs. Al Dove. "You used to know her, didn't you, Cagey?" Freddy Schwartz had asked, and when I didn't answer: "Back when she was Binty Banks? Weren't you and she something of a number once?"

"I used to know her," I'd said finally. "But who's behind it?"

"I'm just coming to that. All it cost you was a trip to the Hall of Records. Al and Binty Dove are the listed officers, but you'll never guess who owns the property."

"Who owns the property, Freddy?"

"Does the Rancho del Cielo Corporation ring a bell?"

It did, and a hell of an obvious one. Rancho del Cielo was the real estate swindle Al Dove had been involved in a few years back. It had been one of those desert retirement paradises which pop up like cholla cactus all over Southern California, with golf course and clubhouse and door-to-door morticians, so much down and the rest in your will. Only the pine they'd built Rancho del Cielo out of was so green you could hear the sap hissing and the financing had turned out to be as creaky as the suckers who'd bought in. And Al Dove and his partners had gotten out two steps ahead of the scandal and about half a step ahead of the Law.

Freddy Schwartz named the partners from memory. Most of them I recognized. Put together they spelled mob. This was nothing new for Al Dove, but the art connection sure was for the mob. I asked Freddy about it.

"I've had trouble pinning it down, Cagey. It seems there's quite a traffic in stolen pictures, a booming one I understand, but a lot of it works through the insurance outfits. I mean, they rip off a big collector and then they try to deal with the insurance boys. And the insurance boys cough up mostly. I did some digging for you down at the paper, there're some photocopies already in the mail to you. But nobody connects the gallery to it."

" 'A lot of it,' you said. But what about the stuff that doesn't go back through the insurance companies?"

"I'm not there yet. Maybe it goes up for sale, but outside the U.S.? Who knows, maybe through your friend Dove in Paris? I'm betting they ship out the stuff that's not covered by insurance."

"But why wouldn't it all be insured?"

"Maybe because some of it's already hot."

"What does that mean?"

"Just what you think it means. I understand there's a

whole underground market in hot art. It's dealt all over the world, on the quiet, and it seems the most respectable collectors are into it."

The way I read it, Al Dove's partners must have gotten into art the way they'd gotten into a lot of other so-called legitimate businesses: for investment and diversification. They'd used Al Dove as a front man before, and even though he'd meant trouble for them before, well, like I said, you work with what you've got. And probably it had even been legitimate . . . in the beginning. Only Al Dove's partners, being business-men, had gotten greedy, and being men of habit, had taken to stealing their wares instead of buying them. And had organized themselves accordingly. With a branch in Paris for what they couldn't unload in America. Because in Paris, as Bernard Lascault had put it, nobody asked too many questions.

But what had gone wrong? Had somebody begun to ask questions, and if so, who? According to Bernard Lascault, the market was soft and Al Dove lacked con-trol. But control of what?

I'd asked Freddy Schwartz about forgeries. He hadn't heard anything about forgeries. I'd asked him about Helen Raven and William Rillington, and about a brother called Jonnison Davis. At first the names meant nothing to him. Then suddenly, when I went on to John Blumenstock, one of them did.

"You remember it, don't ya, Cagey? It was in the courts, all the papers carried it. Blumenstock's widow versus his girl friend? Over who got custody of the paintings?"

"Wait a minute, Freddy. What paintings?"

"Who knows what paintings? *Paintings!* Blumenstock's paintings. Helen Raven, she was the girlfriend.
She was with him when he drove off a cliff. No, it
wasn't a cliff. A bridge? Yeah, a bridge, I think that's
right. And she came out of it scarred for life. She
showed up in court still wearing the bandages. Look,
I'll dig it all out for you, Cagey. I'll . . ."

"Okay, Freddy. But who won?"

"Who won what?"

"The court case."

"Who won the court case? Why she did, Helen
Raven, wouldn't it figure?"

And to think he carried all that around in his little
jewish noodle.

Freddy Schwartz had had something else to tell me.
I'll get to it in due course. Meanwhile, once I'd left the
gendarme holding up the entrance at Al Dove's, I had
a couple of phone calls of my own to make, and I
ducked into a café at the big circle at the corner.

The first one was to that cute little apartment I've
mentioned up under the eaves in Montparnasse.
They're a strange breed, the girls from Air France:
they've nothing against a little promiscuity . . . so long
as it's in the family. So that when Josiane answered the
phone and wanted to know where I'd been and I said
I'd been in jail, she hung up on me, and it took another
call, complete with recriminations and apologies, for
me to get what I wanted.

The second went much more smoothly. I'd "read"
the two numbers when La Ducrot tapped them out,
but all I knew about them was that they were both

somewhere outside Paris. I didn't get any answer at the first one either, but my spiel to the flunkey who answered at the second went something like this:

"Allo? This is Mr. Magnavox speaking from the International Department of American Express? I wonder if you can help me? We're holding a transfer of funds for a Lascault, Edouard, of Rambouillet in the Yvelines, that's Lasc . . . what's that? Pardon me? You said *Bernard* Lascault? Lascault, *Bernard*? Imagine that! Who could have made such a mistake? But could I have your address please? . . . Yes, is that near Rambouillet in the Yvelines? . . . No? Where? *Chantilly*? . . . But that's nowhere near Rambouillet, is it? . . . A-*hah*! I knew there had to be a confusion in our records, please forgive me for . . . what's that? Ah yes, thank you, thank you very kindly . . ."

I hung up, patted myself on the back, and after a fast croque monsieur and a Löwenbrau in the sunshine of the café terrace, the Giulia and I were off to the races. Nor were we alone. Maybe he'd been with us all morning, but I first picked him up in Al Dove's street, a white 204 coupe with Paris plates and nothing whatsoever remarkable about him.

SIX

THE WOODS AROUND CHANTILLY are full of people with six-figure incomes camping out in mansions that wouldn't look out of place, say, in Marin County or Bel Air. And maybe this would be impressive enough on its own, if it wasn't for the fact that they've got neighbors who can earn that kind of loot in a couple of minutes on a Sunday afternoon. The only notable difference between the two groups is that one is two-legged and the other four, and you'd be hard put to say which outswanks which. To give you an idea, the racetrack, which is the prettiest I've ever seen, is on the grounds of the château itself, and the winner's purse in the Prix du Jockey in June makes the Kentucky Derby look like nickel-raise poker. All you can eat, servants to tend to your every need, and retirement at four to a lifetime of fucking, now who among us would turn that down?

My knowledge of the area, I confess, pretty much

began and ended with the track, and it took me quite
some jiggling and questioning before I located the
Lascault hideaway. This gave my friend in the 204
coupe fits. I drove clean through their hamlet once
and out the other side, then had to turn around and
head back in. We passed each other in the middle of
the village. He looked at me and I at him, a nondescript guy in a nondescript car. I waved to him.
Then I found a local peasant who directed me to a
discreet stone wall with a wooden gate in it, tucked
down a narrow alley behind the baker and the butcher,
and a moment later I was piloting the Giulia through
the seigneurial domain.

I don't know what else to call it. The house of course
was enormous. Or at least I took it for the house, until I
found out it belonged to the gatekeeper. The main
house was considerably further along a paved road, a
stately stone manse half-hidden by the trees, not very
old by French standards, maybe a century or so, but
beautifully proportioned and landscaped, with fans of
trees on either wing and a great expanse of rolling
lawn dipping away from the entrance. Majestic as the
house was, though, it was the grounds that really
popped my eyeballs. The French would have called it a
park, and rightly so. All along the road were handsome stands of poplars, just beginning to leaf overhead. Behind them was lawn and more trees, but these
planted and shaped to form perfect geometries, circles, and ovals of shade against the sunswept turf.
There were spring flowers in abundance, planted in
great stone urns close to the house itself, and within
the circle formed there by the road I saw beds of iris on

the verge of bursting. Somewhere was a pond with swans, somewhere else what looked like a rosery, with a stone-arbored walk down the center.

And no one in sight, not a soul.

Either Madame Lascault had a pair of very green thumbs, I thought, or the art business was a lot more booming than her husband had let on.

I got out of the Giulia. She looked pretty grubby in those surroundings. I had the feeling I did too. I rang the front bell, and a vassal in immaculate livery let me in. When I stated my business, he took my card, ushered me into a sun-filled drawing room with a wide bay window bellying over the rear lawn and assorted outbuildings, then left me to study signatures.

Of these there were plenty, and a few would have been familiar to me even before I started my lessons in art history. Every inch of wall space, it seemed to me, was hung with paintings, as though their owner couldn't bear to stick a few away in a closet. It didn't seem in the best of taste—the walls had a way of crowding you, and you couldn't begin to look at one picture before the one above it, or below, took your eye away— but I suppose you and I might do the same if we had all those Picassos lying around. So I concentrated on the signatures, and several of them turned out to be Blumenstocks, and there was even one I kind of took a shine to, though I'd be hard pressed to say why. All it was was a diagonal slash that went across the canvas from lower left to upper right, where it broke off in a hook. The slash was in a pale sort of blue. I thought it was a pretty nice color.

"It's beautiful, isn't it, Mr. Cage?" said a cultured

voice behind me, in English. It was high-pitched, strong. I thought I might have recognized it from La Ducrot's office.

I turned around.

"You *are* American, aren't you?"

It took me a long minute to get out anything at all. Remember that at the time I had no idea who Madame Bernard Lascault was, or had been. All I knew, right then, was that I'd seen her. And I knew it instantly. I even think the idea of it, the premonition, struck me a split second before I actually saw her. It was a shock all right, the more so because I'd never seen her in the flesh, only sitting erect on a garish purple couch, larger-than-life-sized, in a lime-colored gown and tur-baned, and a set of spotlights shining on her startled face.

She was wearing a long-sleeved gray jersey dress which came down to mid-calf. Her hair was gray-blond, shoulder-length, and not a strand out of place. Her face was long, her features sharply outlined. She had tight lips, a sharp straight nose, hazel eyes. She must have been in her mid-fifties and it showed, in the mottled skin of her hands and some dark, precadaver-ous hollows around her eyes. Her posture was what I could only call aristocratic. She was tall and thin to begin with, and she carried her shoulders thrust slightly forward, which concaved her chest and elon-gated her curving spine. It gave her a long-stemmed, titless look, one I associate with dames from the upper crust, and to such an extent I suspect they practice it in front of mirrors. No beauty at all, Madame Bernard

Lascault, but a certain class—if you go for the class.

"*Excusez-moi*," she said in a strongly accented French, "*je vous ai pris pour un Américain.*"

"That's all right, Mrs. Lascault," I said finally. "I'm American."

"I don't believe we've had the pleasure . . . ?"

"No," I said, "I don't believe we have."

"Then what can I do for you? Won't you sit down?"

I sat down. She sat across from me. It was improvising time, but my imagination was galloping a couple of city blocks ahead, even though all I had for sure was that a dead painter had painted her portrait with a man who wasn't her current husband. He'd done her justice too, in a cruel sort of way. Except that the picture had been called a fake.

I told her I'd really come to see her husband, and the interview almost ended right there. She stiffened at the name. Her chin lifted angrily. She said he wasn't home. She started to stand up. The telephone shrillness was in her voice, and her posture, suddenly stiff and erect, reminded me of the painting.

"Look, Mrs. Lascault," I said, staying put, "I don't know to what extent you're aware of it, but some pretty unpleasant things have been going on lately in your husband's field." I ticked them off on my fingers. "People have been beaten up, the police have been impersonated, there's been a man murdered. Others have disappeared, nobody seems to know where to, and as far as the Paris police are concerned, they seem strangely uninterested."

I started over at the thumb when I ran out of fingers, but the more I went on, the more she seemed to relax, and her body subsided into the chair, a high-backed modern affair in white molded foam.

A curious reaction.

I looked at the wall behind her, at the pale blue diagonal slash.

"I take it somebody here is specially interested in Blumenstocks. Would that be Mr. Lascault?"

"They belong to me," she answered firmly, pinching her lips together. "*Everything* you see here is mine." I caught the emphasis, but then her voice went languid. "But enough pleasantries, Mr. Cage. Whom are you working for? For Alan Dove, I suppose?"

"I thought I was working for your husband," I said. Taking the check from my pocket, I smoothed it out on the coffee table between us. I turned it around so that it faced her. She leaned forward.

"You come rather cheap, don't you?" she said. "But at least you were paid. What did he hire you to do?"

"There were some people he wanted me to investigate for him."

"What people?"

I thought about it for a moment.

"Alan Dove, in fact," I said. "Also a woman called Helen Raven."

"Alan . . . ?" she began. She started to laugh, then caught herself. The shrillness was back in her tone. "And what did you find out?"

"You'll excuse me, Mrs. Lascault, but I think that should be between me and your husband."

"Oh?" She started again, like the dame in the picture. "It's a professional secret, is it?"

"Something like that."

"But *he* hired you to investigate . . . *them?*"

"That's right."

The surprise in her expression gave way to a smile. Not a nice smile.

"Well," she said, "I don't think it matters, Mr. Cage. I don't think he'd be particularly interested in what you found out. Not at all. In fact I don't think he'd give a damn, not the slightest damn. Or anyone else. You've wasted your time, Mr. Cage. Too bad, I'm sure it was valuable. But it's all over, the whole disgusting affair."

This was the same message I'd heard from the Law the night before. Only this time, with a suddenness I hadn't expected, it overflowed into something else.

"So what did you find out?" she shrilled at me. "Never mind! You don't have to tell me, let me guess! You found out that Alan Dove and his wife are petty crooks, didn't you? Didn't you find that out? A pair of cheap chiseling opportunists? You didn't have to bust your balls to find it out, did you? And Helen Raven . . ."

Her voice broke into a raucous scorn.

". . . that fraudulent whore. I bet you feel sorry for her too. Don't you? All the world feels sorry for Helen, why would you be any different? Poor, scarred Helen, that bitch-cunt. Did you put your nose into her, Mr. Cage? I bet you got down on all fours and put your nose into her. Disgusting! But that's how you find out about Helen, Mr. Cage, you have to snuffle her like a pig! Well, but at least you got paid for it, didn't you?

Otherwise you'd have stolen your pay, Mr. Cage. You can't fool me. *I* could have told him all you found out in two minutes. That cheap sucking whore, she . . ."

She stopped cold, as if she'd only just heard what she was saying. But then, hearing it, she started to laugh. And then:

"Tell me, Mr. Cage, did you find out the big secret? *The biggest secret of all?*"

But the laughter took her again. It shook her in gusts, grating, vindictive, and her body gave way to it like stones cracking in an avalanche. She tried to talk through it, something about her husband, about there being no honor among thieves, but then she started to cough instead. The coughing wracked her, twisted her. She jerked forward. I thought she was going to plunge onto the table, but she caught herself as quickly, and coughed violently, and pulled a handkerchief from her sleeve, blew hard, twice, and rocked back, and her eyes darted like she was looking for something to throw. The air in the room trembled and seethed. I prepared to duck. Instead her eyes lit on my check, Bernard Lascault's check. She seized on it in triumph. Laughing again, she ripped it down the center. Then she ripped the two pieces down the center savagely, and the four after that. Then when she couldn't rip any more—there's a limit, even when your muscles are popping with meanness—she let fly, loosing her clenched fist over the coffee table in a shower of paper shreds.

We watched them spray down: my first earned income in how many moons?

She wasn't laughing any more.

"Don't worry about it, Mr. Cage," she said coldly. "*I'll* pay you for your work."

Unlike other semihysterical binges I'd witnessed, though, there was no visible release for her in it. She'd fought for control and won it, but in the process her body had gone stiff like petrified wood. Her chin was up, her eyes sunken, immobilized.

"Do you know what they want from me, Mr. Cage?"

When I didn't say anything, she answered herself: "Two million francs. Two million francs, that's a great deal of money for three paintings, wouldn't you say? Between four and five hundred thousand dollars? Two of which paintings have never been offered for sale and the third of which was once withdrawn from auction for lack of an acceptable offer?"

It was, I thought, a great deal of money under any circumstances.

"Do you know what the top bid was for it then, Mr. Cage? Twelve thousand dollars. The top bid and the only bid."

"Did *you* make it, Mrs. Lascault?" I asked.

She didn't seem to hear the question. I wanted to ask too if she'd stolen it instead, or had had it stolen, and a lot of other things that were percolating in my brain, but her eyes were a thousand miles away. Or years. Whatever she was seeing made her lips tighten a little harder. The color squeezed out of them, and her cheekbones took on the sheen and pallor of a death mask.

She broke out of it finally.

"Two million francs. That was the price, Mr. Cage. Either that or they'd be sold on the open market." With a half-snort she tossed her head, and the gray-blonde of her hair flipflopped gently before falling back into place. "I want those paintings, Mr. Cage. I'll tell you what I'm prepared to pay now. Five hundred thousand. Francs, that is. Five hundred thousand francs for three paintings. Notice that I said *three*. No more, no less. That too is my top bid and my only bid. Five hundred thousand francs. And under the circumstances I'd say it was an extremely generous one, wouldn't you agree?"

"Particularly if one of the three is a fake, yes, I would."

She looked at me appraisingly. Her eyelids drooped slightly and her lashes seemed to quiver. Otherwise the room right then was as still as a morgue.

"I think we understand each other," came her reply.

Even though I didn't, not yet, I was ready then to admire her style. At least she was a woman who knew what she wanted and what she was prepared to pay to get it. That takes a certain class. But then she had to go and ruin the image.

"You strike me as a clever man, Mr. Cage," she said. "I take it you didn't come here to see my husband, not at all. Obviously. Still, I think you deserve some compensation for your efforts. Let me make you a proposition then."

She glanced down at the bits of paper on the coffee table. They made her smile. It was her second smile of the day and, as I recall, the last one I ever saw.

"We'll put it on a perfectly business basis," she said. "My offer, as I've told you, is five hundred thousand francs. You can simply pass that along if you like, in which case I'll pay you double what my husband paid you. But if you prefer, I'd be happy to let you negotiate within that ceiling. Let's agree that . . . half? . . . yes, why not half? . . . of whatever you save me will be yours to keep?"

Normally I'm not averse to propositions, at least to listening, but the half stuck in my craw. And maybe if she'd pulled out her checkbook right then, I'd have torn it up too. But she didn't, needless to say. People like that don't pay up front. Instead she was already on her feet, shoulders forward, her hand extended.

What is it about the rich that makes you let them get away with it? Or is that why they're rich?

I said something to the effect that I'd think her proposition over. I took her hand. It was limp in mine and cold all right, like ice.

SEVEN

I swung out past the gatehouse. I didn't look back. The guy in the white 204 was waiting for me, picking his nose behind the wheel. He was about as inconspicuous as a Good Humor truck in a village that size. I didn't wait for him to free his finger either, and it wasn't till I neared the autoroute that I slowed down for him.

I've a theory about tails and the people who hire them. If they're that interested in knowing where I'm going, then I'd as soon they knew . . . till the right time comes. Otherwise they get nervous and fidgety, and people who hire tails are nervous enough already. So it wasn't to save his job that I took it easy on the autoroute, and when he almost lost me coming off at Clignancourt, I stopped by a kiosk and made a show of buying a newspaper till he picked me up again. He was with me at the hotel, then someone else took over that night in Montparnasse, and the next time I spotted the

first one he'd traded in the Peugeot for a navy blue
Renault 5 and he was working on his ear with a
Q-tip.

By that time, though, it mattered even less. Or ought
to have. I'd decided to take the Law's advice. Circumstances partly beyond my control had put me into the
middle of an ugly situation. From what I learned that
night in Montparnasse, it was probably going to get
uglier. For my pains I'd had a lesson in why the rich are
rich, salutary maybe, but Mrs. Bernard Lascault could
find herself another messenger. And as for the other
side of it, well, he'd said it himself, hadn't he? *I owe you
one, baby. I'm going to pay you back and then we'll be quits.*
Sure Al, and good luck with your two million, and send
me a postcard from paradise.

In other words, I was like Rip Van Winkle, only if
Mr. Van Winkle had woken up in the late twentieth
century and taken a look around, chances are he'd
have gone back to sleep.

Or tried to.

I'm going to tell you a story now. In many ways it's an
exemplary tale, and it'll go a long way toward filling in
the gaps. It did mine. I heard it that night, or most of it,
up under the eaves in Montparnasse, from the guy I'd
asked Josiane to invite over for a drink, a fellow coun-
tryman called Elliott Grunen. Elliott Grunen, I should
say, wasn't my type, and I never could see what the Air
France mafia saw in him, except maybe a certain bisex-
ual ingenuity. He was one of those professional
America baiters who'd come to Europe years ago with
an ample inheritance, which he'd been squandering
ever since on a variety of fancy no-capitals publications

nobody read. One of them, however, was, or had been, a slick bilingual affair called *l'amateur d'art* in French and *the art lover* in English. Elliott Grunen, I figured, ought to know just what I was after, and in this I was very right.

The story then:

Once upon a time when our country was younger and richer, the art center of the western world was a small and seedy corner of New York City known as the East Village. Thousands of would-be paintpushers came there from all over, lured by a bunch of artists who'd already staked out the territory and were just then making it big, men with some of those double-play-combination names I've cited, like Pollock, Gorky, deKooning, Kline. Taken together, they were known as the Abstract Expressionists. According to their boosters, they'd made a revolution, and some of them were still around to tell about it, in the proverbial cold-water flats and lofts which now had steam heat, and holding court in a local joint called the Cedar Tavern to a whole horde of camp followers. Among these was a young aspirant from the Midwest called John Blumenstock.

John Blumenstock, though, had three strikes against him when it came to making it in that scene: 1) he was a serious painter; 2) his personality; 3) he took his masters straight. The work he turned out in those days was directly in the Abstract Expressionist line. Probably it was testament to how good he was that he got any notice at all, because nobody could care less about a second generation of painters when the living legends of the first were just beginning to pull down big money for their production. The more so when the second generation was a private, slack-jawed, quiet kid who earned his bread working as a clerk-typist on Wall Street. According to Elliott Grunen, other artists praised his work even then, and it had been shown in group shows, but to the public he was unknown, to the art hucksters he was a hopeless case, and if history had been left to its course, he might one day have ended up a footnote, in one of those slick no-capitals magazines nobody reads.

As it was, he got discovered.

Her name was Judith Springberg, people in the know called her "Cookie," and even I had heard of the family, if not this particular member. Like most jews who crossed the ocean early enough, the Springbergs had made their pile more than once, and in more than one way. Later on, the sources of their loot went mostly anonymous—it's safer that way, for taxes as well as anti-Semitism—but for all those Springberg heirs to devote their lives to the best causes, you know they've got it stashed away somewhere.

In any case, Cookie Springberg's chosen cause was Art. Or rather: Artists. To hear Elliott Grunen tell it, she'd been born with a checkbook between her legs and at one time or another she'd tried to buy them all. She too was a habitué of the Cedar Tavern scene; she too had gotten to be a legend in her own time. But once they'd used her, once they'd been fed and sheltered and sucked and suckled by Cookie Springberg, the artists left her dry, with nothing to show for it, so the legend went, but a shrill voice and jangled nerves and, along the way, a collection that would have had most museum directors slavering outside the service entrance of her mansion.

She was thirty-six and John Blumenstock twenty-eight when they got married. Put charitably, it was love at second sight; put Elliott Grunen's way, they were each other's last hope. Because if Cookie Springberg bought Blumenstock, she also made him. Overnight the good painter became the great young American painter. Even what had worked against him before turned to glamour in her hands. That he was shy or private made him a man of mystery. That he'd stuck to Abstract Expressionism when others had dropped it made him courageous. That he was Midwestern Protestant made him vintage American, like corn on the cob. Suddenly here was a genuine home-grown product, tailor-made for the media. His first one-man exhibition, in the right gallery on New York's 57th Street, was sold out before it opened.

They stayed together some six years, a fertile period as far as his work was concerned. But then, at least according to the official history, John Blumenstock blew it all. He took to booze, then to dope. He wrecked one friendship after another, and what little work he did was sheer fad-following. The villain of the piece, the one responsible for his downfall, was an aggressive and opportunistic young art critic. Her name? Helen Raven. It was Helen Raven who'd pushed him into disastrous experimenting, Helen Raven who'd run through his fortune, Helen Raven who'd driven him in the end to suicide. Because if the cause of death had gone down in the books as accidental, it was common knowledge that Blumenstock had driven his car off a bridge in a drunken rage, and the fact that Helen Raven had been the one to survive, with only a face scarred for life once they'd finished picking the windshield out of it, was just the last irony in the tragedy.

The only trouble with the official history, as passed on by Elliott Grunen, was that its author was Cookie Springberg Blumenstock. Because from what I knew as well as some of the things Grunen said, there were other ways of looking at it. In any case, for several years after his death, Helen Raven had had to fight in the courts for possession of the late Blumenstocks. Cookie was his widow, and since he'd left no will, she claimed the entire estate. It had been a bloody battle, it must have been an expensive one, and the winner had come away with a handful of paintings nobody wanted. Because if Helen Raven had managed to prove ownership, at least to the satisfaction of her judges, Cookie had thereupon set out to discredit the late work in every way she could, as only she could.

"But were they any good?" I asked Elliott Grunen.

"The late Blumenstocks?" He made a face. "Careless, I'd say. Of course he'd gone representational. They were interesting. He had tremendous vitality, even then. Of course I've only seen one. In recent years, that is."

"The one that's been in the papers?"

"That's right. The self-portrait. Of course I was there the other night." (And of course it was like him to let you know such things.)

"But that one's a fake, isn't that what they're saying?"

He smiled knowingly. "Of course a lot of things are

called fake these days. If it's a fake it's a very good one."

"How many are there?" I asked him.

"How many of what?"

"Of the late Blumenstocks."

"I wouldn't know. Only a few. I don't think anyone knows exactly. Of course Helen Raven would, she lived with him. But since when are you into art? I wouldn't have thought it was your bag."

His smile veered off into condescension . . .

"It's not," I said. "I was more interested in Cookie."

. . . to disappear into surprise. "Oh? You mean the eminent Mrs. Lascault?"

"That's right," I said, grinning back at him. "I just met her this afternoon."

It was almost dawn when Air France took off and the Giulia and I drove home down the Rue d'Assas. The way it looked to me, Al Dove and Helen Raven had joined forces to shake Cookie Springberg Blumenstock Lascault's money tree, conceivably with Bernard Lascault's help. Only Cookie Lascault wasn't having any part of it, and maybe she'd even gone so far as to hire her own private army of phony Law to prove the point. From what I'd gathered, the portrait of her and Blumenstock probably wasn't a fake, but it had been pretty astute to call it one in public—a million and a half francs' worth of astuteness, if you wanted to look at it that way. I hadn't seen it that afternoon, but I was willing to bet it was already somewhere in the Chantilly mansion, and the only reason Al Dove still had a shot at half a million francs was that she wanted the other ones that went with it.

Well, I said to the Giulia on the way back to the hotel through the quiet streets, good luck to them all.

Sure I said it. Sure, sure, and triple sure.

But there was another element in the equation. Freddy Schwartz had mentioned it. He hadn't been the only one. It had been on my mind that night in Montparnasse even after Grunen left, and it came again in the silent pre-dawn, and again when I woke up later on. Like I've said, not even all the skills of Josiane and her mates had ever managed to erase it altogether. So that I had no call to be surprised, and in fact I wasn't. Only shook. The big shakes, the ones inside that you never get rid of entirely.

I was, of all places, lying in my tub. It was a big tub, big enough for me and all my rubber ducks and sailboats, and the water came out so hot it all but peeled the enamel off the tiles. I'd ordered breakfast, and when the knock came at the door, I figured it for the chambermaid with the tray. And so it was. But she wasn't alone, and the voice in the bathroom doorway spoke to me across a gulf of five years:

"Hello, Cagey. Will you tell her to bring another pot of coffee?"

The skin at the back of my neck prickled and tingled. I called out to the chambermaid. I heard her *"Oui, Monsieur,"* and then the door to my suite shut.

I turned around.

She was about as I'd pictured her in my mind, so much so it was uncanny. The last time I'd seen her, in fact, she'd been asleep in a bed, the sheet tangled over her, but I'd carried around another image of her, a pretty corny one at that but you live with what you live with. The image was of palm trees blowing in the wind. I saw her with her back into the wind, and the wind blowing her hair off the neck and spraying it forward around her face. I don't know where it came from— there's not much wind in L.A. and less in a hotel bathroom in St. Germain-des-Prés—but that's what I saw again, in the doorway . . . for a split second.

There wasn't much to her. There never had been. The only difference I could detect were some lines around the eyes when she smiled. They did her no harm. She was wearing an off-white raincoat, unbuttoned, with the belt hanging loose on either side and her hands in her pockets.

"Have I changed that much?" she said, one cheek lifting in a sheepish sort of grin.

"No, Binty," I answered. "Not at all, I'd say."

"You're not doing so bad yourself," she said, laughing. There was that too, the laugh that was pitched lower than her voice, husky, pleasing if you go for husky laughter.

I had once.

By this time I was standing up in the tub and reaching for a towel. I told her I'd be with her in a couple of minutes, that the chambermaid would bring her coffee, that we'd have breakfast together. But she stayed in the doorway, watching me while I shaved. She always had—that is to say, during that week or so of her life—and she knew, I suppose, that I'd remember, and that the memory would unnerve me whether I showed it or not. It did, and I didn't.

We had breakfast in the sitting room, I in my bathrobe and nothing else, Binty Dove in her raincoat with
a sweatshirt and a pair of jeans underneath. Or rather:
I had breakfast and Binty Dove watched me eat.

Binty Dove said: "I suppose you're surprised to see
me, Cagey."

"Not really. I'd heard you were in Paris."

"Who told you?"

"A little birdie."

"And do you know why I've come to see you?"

"More or less. You want me to bail Al out of trouble
again."

The laugh again, husky. "You don't forget, do you."

"Sure I forget. Like just until this min . . ."

"Or bear grudges either."

"No, of course not. No grudges. You did what you
wanted to do. You saw how to do it and you did it."

"I did what I wanted to do?" she repeated, slowly.
"And that's all?"

"That's all. That's all she wrote."

She looked me in the eye. "You lousy son of a bitch,"
she said flatly.

"Sure," I said, "the guy who gets played for a sucker
is always the lousy son of a bitch."

"You weren't played for a sucker, Cagey. No, that's
not true. You're right. You were, in a way. But I tried
to explain. I wanted to explain."

"After you'd walked?"

"I couldn't face you. But I called you. I don't know
how many times I called."

"I got the message."

"But you didn't call back, Cagey. I even wrote you a letter."

"Yeah," I said, "but you didn't send me an invitation to the wedding."

"Did you read my letter?"

"No," I said. "I tore it up."

It was the truth. I remembered doing it.

Her head dropped. She held her chin in her hand and her hair sprayed forward over her face. Maybe if we'd had it out five years before, I thought in passing, things would have been different. More likely, that was what she wanted me to think in passing. I had my doubts. A lot of things change in five years. So they say.

"Look, Binty," I said. "You didn't come here to talk over old times. What's on your mind?"

She looked up at me, dry-eyed.

"Believe what you want to, Cagey," she said. Her head was at a slight angle, but she fixed me with her eyes. "Al and I are washed up. Finished. All she wrote, like you said. For quite a while, believe it or not, it's been only business between us. Now that's gone too."

She paused, as though waiting for a reaction.

"Gee," I said gallantly, "that's a nasty break. But..."

"How much do you know about what he's been into lately?"

"Well, enough to say it sounds like a sweet little racket. I understand you're in it with him?"

"I have been."

"As well as some other people he's dummied for in the past?"

"As well as some other people."

"Well," I repeated, "a sweet little racket. And maybe not so little at that."

"No, not so little."

She told me about it then. Essentially it was what I'd already gotten from Freddy Schwartz. The product mix was of hot art and cool all right, but they had a system of laundering the former so that anyone who did start asking the wrong questions would have a hell of a time coming up with the right answers. Very sweet. Al Dove was the front man, he'd made it work at the Paris end, while Binty minded the store in Beverly Hills. To her credit, she didn't fudge on the slimier parts. Nor did she brag when she laid their sales figures on me. She didn't have to. It was more like the chairman of the board delivering the annual report to the faithful.

No, I thought, not so little.

"It sounds pretty great to me," I said. "A sweet operation. So what's gone wrong?"

"Al has."

"How come? Don't tell me he's overextended himself again."

"In a way. You know Al. His expenses went sky high. Then he started dabbling on his own. Badly. It was the wrong time. He lost his shirt."

"Except that it wasn't his shirt?" She didn't answer. She didn't have to. "And then . . . don't tell me, let me guess. He found Helen Raven? Or was it Helen Raven who found him?"

"Al can be a very persuasive person. And Helen Raven's a very misguided woman."

"Misguided? I'd have thought single-minded more than misguided."

"She had some paintings to sell."

"Which, the way I hear it, she hadn't been able to sell before?"

"That's right."

"But Al saw a way of hyping them over here. The only trouble being there weren't enough of them, right? Which is where Rillington must have come in. Whose idea was Rillington, Binty?"

"Rillington was Helen Raven's student. He's also a very gifted young painter."

"I bet he is. Particularly with the right teacher. But what was in it for him? He didn't do it just for love, did he?"

"Al offered to underwrite his career."

"Ahh. Al's always been such a generous guy."

She scowled at me. It was one of her best expressions, eyebrows down, mouth tight with the lower lip jutting.

"And you're so fucking pure," she said. "You've always been so fucking pure."

"Me? Pure?" It was my turn to laugh. "On the contrary, it all sounds very clever to me. You had a shortage of product so you found someone to produce it. The only person in the world who knew how many late Blumenstocks there were was Helen Raven herself. And with Helen Raven on hand to inspire the artist and authenticate the finished product, how could you go wrong? With, in addition, Cookie Lascault as the prospective buyer and her husband to grease the way?"

She didn't contradict me.

Only it had gone wrong. And I was beginning to see why.

"What happened, Binty? Did Al get greedy? How many Blumenstocks has Rillington turned out? Or was it simply that Al decided to go it alone?"

She hesitated, biting down on that lower lip.

"He's got some property that belongs to us," she said. "We want it back."

"Who's *us*?" I said. Then, when she didn't answer: "I bet you do. Including Helen Raven and Rillington?"

She hesitated again. Then she nodded.

"That's right," she said, "them too. Though not for the reasons you think. Al's out, Cagey. We're not going to let him take us all down with him. There's more at stake. There's the whole . . . well, call it what you want to."

I could see that too.

"And so? Don't tell me you want me to find him for you?"

She nodded again.

There was one of those pungent silences.

"It's not like before," she said, averting her eyes. "I asked you to save his neck then. All right, maybe that *was* for my sake. But this time it's strictly business. Whatever happens to Al is strictly his look-out. We're ready to pay you anything you want, in dollars or francs, here or in the States. We're ready to cut you in if that's how you want it." She smiled at me. "If you're not too pure, that is."

This was the third time somebody had tried to hire me that week, and each time the price had gone up. It was very flattering. Probably I should retire more often.

"One thing I've been trying to figure out," I said, "is how Lascault got to me in the first place. I mean, I've been out of action a long time, ever since I got to Paris, yet he knew where to find me and all about my unsavory past. How well do you know Bernard Lascault?"

"We've talked."

"About what to do about Al?"

"Yes, that."

"And so you put him onto me, is that it?"

"Yes I did. Maybe it'll surprise you, Mister B. F. Cage, but I've managed to keep tabs on you."

She looked across at me. Unconsciously she ran her hand through the strands of hair to one side of her face. Then she grinned.

I guess I was surprised.

"All these years," she added softly.

I heard her inhale.

I don't know how to describe what happened next, or how it came about. Probably I shouldn't try either. All I can say is that one minute I was sitting there in my bathrobe, drinking coffee, brainstorming away and fairly crackling with wit and acrimony, and the next we were both on our feet, and there wasn't any breakfast table between us, much less half a decade. She came up to about level with my collarbone. That hadn't changed either. I don't think either of us said much of anything. Her head tilted back. She looked up at me with that shining female expression in her eyes and just a twinkle behind it that said I know that you know that we know that it's all a bunch of shit.

I took her by the scruff. I kissed her, in French.

And so, to put it succinctly, a conversation that had started in the bathtub ended up in bed. And where it had been all wrong one minute, the next it was all right.

Or almost.

EIGHT

BECAUSE THERE'S ALWAYS A KICKER to it, isn't there?

Or, to be exact, the absence of one?

For if I'd had a lovely erection sprouting in the sitting room, by the time we got between the sheets, lo and behold, it was long gone. And not all the devices known to the advanced class at Masters & Johnson would bring it back.

A disconcerting development, to say the least.

"It's like everything else," said Binty, holding my bedraggled member in her hand and shaking her head, "they just don't make 'em like they used to."

She bent over it, her hair in her face.

"Don't give it a second thought, little chap," she told it. "He's just worried about his reputation. Besides, we'll get you in the end, just leave it to Binty."

She kissed it on the head. Then she pushed me back down, and snuggled into my shoulder, and started tracing plans on my chest.

Because she was all full of plans, was Binty. She had

it all worked out. The way she had it figured, the
Blumenstock deal could still go through, once they got
the paintings back. Cookie Lascault had proven a more
formidable customer than anyone had expected—that
was partly Al's fault, he'd overplayed his hand—but
Cookie Lascault could kick and connive all she wanted,
she'd pay in the end. Bernard would see to it. Bernard
knew how to bring her around. Besides, said Binty, the
Blumenstock deal was only small potatoes compared
to the overall operation. The overall operation was
what counted. It had to go on. She and Bernard had
been talking about that for some time. The setup was
intact, and it was pretty near foolproof. A beautiful
setup, said Binty. The only trouble was that, with Al
out of the way, there was a beautiful vacuum right in
the middle of it. The beautiful vacuum had to be filled.
She'd already talked to Bernard about that too, Binty
had. She had an idea of her own, a pretty crazy idea
maybe but he'd had nothing against it in principle. She
didn't think the California people would either. She
didn't want me to say anything either way, not now, not
yet. She knew I was too pure, but what was pure any
more? She knew I was a loner, that I'd never worked
for anybody else, but it wouldn't be like working for
anybody else. The partners were silent, they kept their
hands off. She knew I was retired too, Binty did, but
she thought that was ridiculous. Was I going to spend
the rest of my life in a hotel suite and screwing around
with a bunch of sexpots from the airlines? Besides,
what did a bunch of sexpots from the airlines have on a
red-blooded California girl like her?

By this time she was back up on her knees, the sheet

thrown back. She rocked forward onto her hands. Her head came up over mine, the hair spraying down along her cheeks. Her eyes fixed mine, and I could see the glitter of laughter in them.

"Hooooo," she said mockingly, "you really think I mean it, don't you? Well *don't* you? And why not? D'you think it's so farfetched? You'd be good at it, we'd make a fortune! Only d'you think I'm going to spend the rest of *my* life pining away in California while you're here? Man, you must be out of your cottonpickin' *mind*!"

She boxed me in the face with her titties, then when I snapped for them, danced them out of reach, like plums on a tree. She whooped and yelled and dared me to come play, until I grabbed her wrists and pulled her down on top of me, her body suddenly writhing and slithering in my arms. Pound for pound, she was as strong as they come. She bit and fought, she scratched and hollered and kneed, she didn't give a *damn* about the overall operation, all she wanted was *me*, all she'd ever wanted was *me*, why didn't I *know* that, why was I such a *dummy*? Until, exasperated, I rolled her, pinning her small body under mine, kissing her, because it wasn't playtime any more but one thing leading to another, until she freed her hands and reached . . .

. . . with, however, the same disconcerting result.

"What is it, Cagey?" she said, panting for breath below me. "You're not *that* out of practice, are you?"

Then the skin crinkled near her eyes. She smiled up at me. It didn't matter, she said, she'd still get me in the end. Then she pulled me back down to her and breathed in my ear. She licked. She licked some more, and around to my mouth, into it, out, back to the ear. A little later she started to giggle.

"Well the least you can do, you big bastard," she whispered, "is tell me what the B. F. stands for. You never would, 'member? I've decided there are only two things it could be: Benjamin Franklin and Big Fucking. So come on, tell me now, which one is it?"

I started to laugh too. Yeah, I remembered. Then suddenly, without warning, I felt something letting go inside me while she held me fast, five years' worth of it and maybe a lot more. It was like a ship sliding down the rails at a launching. I felt it go all right, with a whooosh, and nothing I could or wanted to do to stop it. *Splash.* And what do you know? When the answer came burgeoning up from where it had been stuck between our bodies, it was big as life and twice as ambitious.

It was afternoon by the time we left the hotel. Afternoon, I should say, of the following day. In between we stopped the world. We sent out for Glenfiddich and champagne, oysters and chicken Kiev. We had strawberries flown in from California and baklava from a bakery I'd heard about in downtown Beirut. We ate it all in bed, in no particular order or position, although if you've never had oysters fed to you while you're flat on your back, I suggest you try it the next chance you get. At some point Freddy Schwartz called. I told him to call back in the morning, and when he called back— it must have been the morning—I unplugged the phone, stuck it in an envelope, stamped it, and sent it to him by the hotel carrier pigeon. And you could say: *Whoa, Boy! Wa-hoa there! You've been there before, remember?* And sure, I remembered all right. Only the last time it had gone on for a week, give or take a few days, and it had ended with Binty saying to me (in bed, it's true): *My darling man, there's something you've got to do for me.* Whereas this time we put it on a strictly business basis.

The original scheme, she told me, had been to sell three late Blumenstocks quietly, through Al Dove and Arts Mondiaux. Cookie Lascault had been the intended buyer from the beginning. Apparently the Professor was hard up for money, enough to sell to a hated rival and at whatever price they could get. But Al Dove had had a better idea, call it his Rillington promotion. Rillington was Helen Raven's lover as well as protégé, and a painter of enough talent to produce as many late Blumenstocks as the market would take, particularly with the dead man's mistress to vouch for them. For if Cookie Lascault ever got tired of buying, her reputation as a collector was such as to start a whole new vogue. So Al Dove had laid it on the Professor, and greed and vengeance had done the rest.

The first time anybody'd had an inkling of what he was up to, Binty said, came when the invitations to the party were sent out. That hadn't been in the game plan, but it had been too late to do anything about it except for Binty to put Bernard Lascault onto me. They hadn't even known Rillington himself was in Paris until I'd reported it to Commissaire Ravier, who'd reported it to Lascault. Lascault had thereupon panicked, which explained why the Law had given me such a hard time. Then he'd called Binty and Binty had caught the next plane. The ruckus at the party, they'd found out, had been Cookie's doing. The people who'd started it belonged to the same gang as the phony Law who'd ended it. The French called them "parallel police." Actually they worked for one of the political parties, but in between elections and revolutions they hired out to the highest bidder, and it stood to reason that Cookie could afford to pay them well, given the million-and-a-half francs' savings she had in mind.

If Al Dove had gotten away in the confusion that night, he'd had to leave everything behind him. Everything, that is, except the contents of the Canal St. Martin studio, plus the painter himself and Helen Raven. That I'd been there too had been an inconvenience, but only a temporary one. All they'd had to do was make sure I didn't blow the whistle too soon. But Jonnie Davis had been a bigger obstacle. Binty didn't know what had happened, but she guessed that Jonnie Davis had balked at the last minute. His first loyalty, after all, was to the people in California, not to Al Dove. So Al Dove had shot him in the eye for his first loyalty and dumped him in the canal, and it had taken some doing for Bernard to convince the Law to sit on the corpse for a while.

As to Al's whereabouts, Binty thought that less of a problem than I did. For one thing, she doubted he'd have tried to cross a frontier with a vanload of paintings. For another, he'd have to try to make contact with Cookie Lascault sooner or later. They had that end pretty well covered, she said. A third possibility occurred to me too: that Al might have abandoned ship and taken off. But no, she didn't think that likely at all. It wasn't his style, she said. It wasn't Helen Raven's either. Besides, once the California people got wind of what had happened, it would behoove Al to have as much cash as he could get his hands on before he took off. Or tried to. No, Binty said, she was pretty sure he'd be holed up somewhere not very far from Paris, waiting to make his move. We had to find him first.

But when the time came to plug the world back in, she was the one who held back.

"It's funny," she said, reaching toward me, "but now that I'm here . . . that we're here . . . I'm spooked about out there. Just a little. It seems such a long way off, Cagey. Why don't we just forget about it?"

"You can forget about it," I said. I was standing by the bed, nude except for an unbuttoned shirt, and gazing down at her. "Stay here if you want. As long as you want."

"Me?"

"That's right. But you hired me to do a job for you, remember? Sometime in the not-so-distant past, like last night? I think it's time I got started."

"Wait a minute," she said, suddenly jumping up. "You're not going alone. I'm going with you."

I laughed at her. It sounded like something out of a movie, like the line the heroine was supposed to deliver when Randolph Scott buckled on his holster.

"It's too dangerous out there, baby," I answered. "The Indians have pointed arrows."

But she didn't laugh back. She started to get dressed with me. Around in there I began to feel a sort of twinge in my stomach.

"Look Binty," I said, shaking my head. "I don't work that way. You'll have to dig up somebody else. I mean, I'll find Al for you, I'll deliver his head to you on a silver platter if that's how you want it, but I've got to do it my own way."

She stared at me. The twinge came again.

"What are you going to do when you find him?" she said.

"What do you want me to do when I find him?"

She hesitated. I got the feeling—a strange one—that she mightn't have thought of that.

"Nothing," she said finally. "I mean, not if you can help it. Just find him, fix him, and then let us know. I'll take care of it then. All we want is our property. I gave you my address, didn't I?"

"Yes, you did; the phone number too."

"It's an apartment Bernard keeps."

"Yes, so you told me." It was my turn to hesitate, but I said it anyway: "Look Binty, you're not by any chance going a little soft and sentimental over ole Al, are you?"

"No," she said emphatically. "It's just that . . ."

"Just that what?"

She turned to me. Her gaze dropped.

"It's just that he's scared of you, Cagey."

"*Scared*? Who, Al? Of *me*?"

"That's why I put Bernard onto you in the first place. I thought you might scare him off."

"Scare him off? Are you kidding?"

Her eyes came up to mine.

"You don't know him, Cagey," she said. "Not at all. He's scared to death of you. He always has been."

In the end we compromised. I let her go with me as far as a café on the Boulevard St. Germain. When we got out on the street outside the hotel, she took my arm. She said the sun was bothering her eyes. It was bright and we'd been indoors for over twenty-four hours, but the Paris sun is never that bright.

She was better at the café. We sat on the sidewalk and watched the world go by. She ordered a croque monsieur and I had a croque madame and we washed them down with chilled Muscadet. But then it was time for me to go to work, and when I told her what I had in mind she got the jitters again.

"Here's what's going to happen," I said to her. "I'm going to pretend like I'm going to the john. You're going to sit here, say, another five minutes, like you're waiting for me to come back. Then you're going to pay the bill and leave."

"What do you mean? What's going to happen to you?"

"Don't make a big deal of it and don't turn around, but the two gents who've been following me are standing inside at the bar. I spotted them coming out of the hotel. They're pretty harmless, I'd say, but it's time I found out who's paying them."

She didn't like the idea at all, though. The panic button was lit in her eyes. She took my hand, squeezed it, hard.

"Unless you are?" I said on a hunch.

She shook her head.

"Or Bernard?"

No, not Bernard either.

She gripped my hand harder. Suddenly I had the impression she couldn't get any words out. That wasn't like her, not at all.

"Look," I said, "just do what I told you. Stay here about five minutes, drink some more wine, then pay the waiter and leave. Take a taxi, go back to Lascault's apartment. Double-lock the door if you're worried. Then wait for me to call."

She nodded, tight-lipped.

"Kiss me again," she managed in a low voice.

"I can't," I said, grinning and freeing my hand as I stood up, "I'm only going to the john."

I went inside to the bar. The telephone and the toilets were downstairs and to get there I had to pass my two friends. Predictably they ducked their heads over their glasses as I went by. Like I said, I'd spotted them when we came out of the hotel, sitting side by side in the navy blue Renault 5, and I'd been surprised at first to see the two of them together. But then I'd realized what a long wait they'd had, and I'd figured I ought to apologize.

What they had no way of knowing, though, was that there was a second way out of the café cellar. Another set of stairs came up past the curve in the bar, out of their line of vision. I went down one flight and up the other and out between the tables onto the side street. A couple of minutes later I was sitting behind the wheel of the Renault 5, rummaging in the shelves under the dashboard until I found what I was looking for.

I copied the name and address off the registration,

then walked leisurely back to the Boulevard St. Germain. Instead of returning to our café, though, I crossed to another one on the shady side, where I found a good seat, about fourth-row center.

Binty was just paying the waiter when I sat down. I watched her get up and cross to the edge of the sidewalk, a small pale face in a raincoat with one arm waving out into the traffic. An empty cab shot across the boulevard to get her, leaving minor mayhem in his wake, and at the same time the two tails burst out of the café. They looked like they were arguing. One of them—my nosepicking friend—jumped inconspicuously into a trailing cab, while his partner did a 360-degree every-which-way neck swivel on the sidewalk. Then I lost him when he disappeared back into the gloom of the café, to pick him up again a moment later when he emerged onto the side street. He looked my way, then the other, and then he took off, running like hell.

NINE

I DON'T BELIEVE in telepathy, and if anxiety's sometimes contagious, the gnaw in my guts when she'd gone
off could as well have been gas.

Or love.

I sat in the café on the shady side of the boulevard,
trying to add it all up. Some of the totals came out
right, some of them didn't. But whatever she might
have fudged on earlier, the panic had been real
enough. In her grip, in her eyes.

Then why the hell'd you send her off by herself? said the
inner voice. Because I only ride alone, I answered;
haven't you ever heard of Lonesome Cage? The inner
voice snickered. *Then stop worrying about it, lover boy.
She's a big girl now, she can take care of herself.*

The first call I made, though, when I went back to
the hotel, was to the number she'd given me to Lascault's private pad. It took me a couple of tries to get
through, and then I plugged into Bernard Lascault's

voice, asking me in French, then in English, to leave a message after the first beep. I heard the first beep. I couldn't think of anything to say to Bernard Lascault. I heard the second beep and hung up.

She'd been caught in the traffic, I told myself.

I dialed the Chantilly mansion. I played it straight this time, and it got me nowhere. Madame was indisposed and not to be disturbed. No, Monsieur wasn't there either, he wasn't expected back until tomorrow. If I cared to leave a message and a phone number . . . ?

I didn't care to.

Then I dialed the pad again, and after a string of busy signals, I broke in on Bernard Lascault's taped voice. I hung up on him and got onto Arts Mondiaux, but it was a Saturday and they must have unplugged the computer. Then I tried my Aunt Minnie in Yakima and a few dozen other people I've known here and there around the globe, trying to make contact somewhere, but the world was out to lunch and it was a hell of a long lunch. Then I tried the pad again, and this time, between the busy signals, a voice came on telling me the number had been changed and giving me another number to dial where they'd give me the new number. Then I tried that other number and got no answer. Then I tried the first number and got a busy signal. Then I banged down the receiver, vowing to send back the next telephone bill unpaid and giving them a number where they could find out my new address, but no sooner had it hit the cradle than with a ring it jumped back into my hand.

"The miracle of modern communications," said

Freddy Schwartz hoarsely, "I never get over it. Six thousand miles away and all you got to do is dial the digits. So? Are you ready to listen this time, Cagey?"

I looked at my watch. It was early morning in California, too early for him to have gotten his edge on. That meant Freddy Schwartz at his long-winded worst. He didn't disappoint me either. He launched into a rambling discourse on crime and inflation. It had gotten so bad a decent citizen was afraid to go outside even if he could afford to. Worse still, the price of Seagram's V.O. had just gone up again. I told him to switch to a cheaper brand, and he said he already had, mostly, which was how he was ruining his liver. I told him not to worry, that I'd already put a check into the mail to him, and he said he'd already gotten it. I told him maybe I'd send him another, and I guess he put the phone down to celebrate the news because when he came back on the sandpaper was gone from his voice.

But all he had to tell me about was Rillington.

"It turns out he's quite the young artist," said Freddy Schwartz. "He's even had a show out here, you'll never guess who put it on." I could, and did. "But what's more, it turns out him and the Raven dame are all mixed up together. He used to be her student and . . ."

". . . now they share the same bed," I finished for him.

"Well how the hell'd you know that?"

"Everybody's doing it, Freddy. So what else you got?"

"It's all tying in for you, Cagey. I had to do a lot of digging, and it wasn't so easy because she's left the country, but d'you know who's she's married to now?"

"Who're you talking about? Helen Raven?"

"Nah, Blumenstock's widow!"

I sighed. I had to listen while he told me all about Bernard Lascault and Arts Mondiaux. Then I asked him if that was all.

"Is that *all*? Well shit, Cagey, that's a hell of a lot of thanks! I've been running all over town for you, I've hardly had an hour's sleep!"

I told him he was doing great. Just great. Only there was something else he could do for me. It was just a little thing—a passing suspicion, say, that wouldn't quite go away.

He seemed to think it was beneath him, though. All of a sudden he was too tired, too old to run around anymore. Why didn't I go get a private eye?

I said I was about to do just that, in Paris. But it ought to be easy for him in L.A. It was just a question of checking passenger lists. If he knew anybody at the airlines, he ought to be able to find out over the telephone.

He said he didn't see what difference it made. I said maybe it didn't make any difference, maybe I was just suspicious by nature. Besides, he said, she was in Paris anyway, wasn't she? He'd already gotten that for me, hadn't he?

"Yeah, I know," I said. "In fact I just saw her."

"Well why don't you ask her?"

"I did," I said.

"Well?"

There was one of those pregnant pauses.

"Listen Freddy," I said, "your check's made out and

the stamps are already dry on the envelope. So cut the shit and just do it for me, will you?"

"You're a white man, Cagey," he said. "I'll call you back."

"You do that," I said.

I told him to put in a good word for me in *shul*, but I think he'd already hung up.

After that I tried the Lascault number one last time, and by a miracle of modern communications I got through . . . to Bernard Lascault again, asking me to leave a message after the first beep.

The concierges of Paris may be legendary gossips, but the two I met that afternoon were about as talkative as a pair of nuns at a circumcision. The first one caught me reading the list of tenants outside her door, on a handsome tree-lined street over in the 15th arrondissement. The gnaw was back in my stomach because the name Lascault was nowhere on the roster. I asked the concierge about him. No, she'd never heard of Monsieur Lascault . . . until I pressed a ten-franc note into her palm. Then she did know him—the apartment, it turned out, was registered in another name—but it cost me another ten to find out that he wasn't there. A third ten brought confirmation that a guest had been using the apartment, yes, a woman, an American, and a fourth that she hadn't seen the American woman since the morning of the previous day. I went upstairs and checked for myself. There was no sound inside, no answer to the buzzer, and the lock on the door was no ordinary hardware. By that time I'd run out of tens, and when I came back down the concierge was wearing that crafty feather-plucking expression the French get when they spot a pigeon. I handed her a fifty, with my card, and told her that if the American woman came back, she was to guard her with her life until they'd contacted me.

The second concierge, by contrast, didn't cost me a centime. This was also in the 15th but a much seedier section of it, where the métro came out of the ground and garbage cans took over from the trees and the music blasting out of the windows was half French rock and half arab singsong. I was a little surprised. I doublechecked the address. It was the one I'd taken off the Renault 5's registration. In any case, and allowing for it losing in translation, my conversation with the building Madonna went something like this:

"I'm looking for Monsieur Fleurie, please."

"Who?"

"Monsieur J.-C. Fleurie?" I said, consulting my notebook. "Fleurie, J.-C.? I believe he's a private investigator?"

"Not here."

"But he lives here, doesn't he?"

"Not in."

"But could you help me locate him? It's important."

"The office."

"The office? Could you tell me where the office is located?"

"*WHO THE HELL DO YOU THINK I AM? THE TELEPHONE DIRECTORY?*"

With that she slammed her door in my face. A moment later, though, the edge of the curtain pulled back from her street-level window. She evil-eyed me as

I got into the Giulia. I sent her back a double whammy
just for luck, because she'd given me a bright idea.

THE EXCEPTIONAL DETECTIVE AGENCY
ELECTRONIC METHODS
ABSOLUTE DISCRETION
ALL CONFIDENTIAL MISSIONS
J.-C. Fleurie, Directeur

had its offices above a cut-rate shoe store over on the
Boulevard de Sebastopol. It's what's called a mixed
commercial district. Nearby, in no particular order,
are the Chatelet theatres, the city hall, the old site of
the Paris markets (currently the world's biggest man-
made hole-in-the-ground) and the Rue St. Denis,
which is the liveliest open-air whorehouse west of
Bangkok. According to the full-column ad in the Paris
yellow pages, the people down at Exceptional Detective would be glad to undertake motorcycle and radio-
car surveillance for you, absolute discretion guaran-
teed, but neither the 204 nor the Renault 5 had had so
much as an antenna and the only electronic equipment
in sight was a small-screen TV on which J.-C. Fleurie,
Directeur, was watching a rugby match when I came
in.

The bigger the ad, you learn in Paris, the seedier the
operation. Exceptional's offices consisted of one
medium-sized room. Two metal desks faced the door,
the vacant one with a typewriter under a plastic cover,
and there were some metal shelves and file cabinets, a
fake-leather two-seater and a couple of metal

armchairs with fake-leather bottoms. A pendulum clock in a wood box hung on the wall, but its hands were pointed respectively at nine and ten and the pendulum had long since given up the ghost. It was the kind of place that lacked only a water cooler to make it homey. Gentle waves of cigar smoke drifted near the ceiling and the TV was turned up full blast to fight the traffic noise.

J.-C. Fleurie, a large and drooping man in a cardigan sweater, waved in the general direction of the metal chairs, then redevoted his attention to the match. I stayed on my feet and watched while the ball squirted out of a roiling mass of bodies. It was lateraled from player to player till it reached the last man near the sideline, who kicked it back into the middle of the field, where it disappeared into another roiling mass. The referee's whistle stopped play.

For some reason the sportscaster seemed to find this a sensational exploit. So did J.-C. Fleurie. He slapped his desk with a meaty palm, exclaiming "*C'est ça, le rugby!*"—at which I leaned across his desk and turned off the set.

He looked up at me, frowning in a hurt, puzzled expression.

"I'm sorry to spoil your fun, Monsieur," I said, "but I want to know where Madame Dove is. I want to know now."

The puzzlement stayed in his dewlaps.

"Madame . . . ?"

"Dove," I said. "D-O-V-E."

"I'm afraid I . . ."

"Of course not. I'm sure you've never heard of her.

Like you've never heard of me either, or had your stooges tailing me for the last few days. Cage is the name, Monsieur. C-A-G-E."

He'd started to stammer something in reply, but at the sound of my name he broke it off. Then to my surprise he beamed broadly. He clapped his hands and stood, his arms spreading wide, and squeezed between the desks, seized my hand and started thumping me on the back.

I freed myself, only for him to take me in a garlic-filled embrace.

"What a pleasure!" he exclaimed. "More than a pleasure, a great honor, Monsieur! To meet an illustrious American colleague! In person! An honor, Monsieur, we'll drink to that!"

He let me go, and pulling open a file drawer, produced a bottle of Pastis, another of water, and a pair of dusty café glasses which he plunked down on the desk. Ahhh, he went on as he poured two measures of the yellow liquid, how he'd always wanted to meet one of us in person, the great ones, Philippe Marlowe, Samu-el Spade, Lewis Archaire—he knew us all by reputation! He asked me if I wanted water and without waiting for an answer, filled both glasses to the brim. Apologizing for the lack of ice, he handed mine across, then with a *"Salut!"* quaffed deeply from his, sighed, smacked his lips, and launched into a florid exposé of the miseries of the investigating profession in France. Because they were only poor cousins in comparison to us, barely eking out a living, working (with a disparaging sweep of his hand) in sordid conditions, I could see for myself, hounded by the authorities, degraded by the press. But was it true what he'd heard about America? That we had offices on the fortieth floors of the skyscrapers? And all that new equipment?—he'd seen it in some film. And whole staffs of girls working for us? Ahhh, he said, kissing his fingertips, the beautiful girls!

I wondered what movies he'd been seeing. In any case, though, there was no stopping him. Because all that new electronic stuff, those high-priced gadgets— they'd been around to try to sell him too, he said, with their fancy catalogues—that was only to impress the clients, wasn't it? Because what good was it to any self-respecting investigator? When it came down to it, was there anything to replace the hard-working investigator with his nose to the ground? Of course not! answered J.-C Fleurie. Times changed, but men didn't!

By this time he'd regained his chair. His cardigan billowed around him. With a glance at mine, he refilled his own glass and produced a pair of cigars.

I shook my head at the cigar and put my glass down on his desk.

"It's been nice meeting you too, Monsieur Fleurie," I said. "Maybe we can swap stories some other time. But right now I need to know where Madame Dove is. If you don't know, one of your boys does. The one who picks his nose."

"Ahhh, Pierrot," he said, and then he chuckled, and then his eyes moistened at a new thought. "You'll have to forgive me, my dear colleague. It is immoral, I know—the height of immorality—for one of us to take an assignment against another. Worse than immoral,

it's an insult to our noble profession! Normally I would
have refused, out of hand. And then, the operatives we
have to work with these days . . . lamentable. Tell me,
how long did it take for you to spot them?"

"Madame Dove, Monsieur," I repeated.

"Ah yes," he said. "Spoken like a true investigator.
Single-minded. Admirable." He paused, nipped the
end of his cigar with his teeth, lit it, then eyed me
through the curling smoke. "But I don't know myself,
Monsieur. I'm a captive to this humble office. Chained
to a desk. In fact I'm waiting for a report myself."

It could have been true. Or he could have been lying
through his rhetoric.

"In that case I'll wait with you," I said. "But there's
one other thing too. Just as one member of the profession to another, of course, but I want to know who's
paying you to keep an eye on me. And her."

"Who's paying . . . ?" he began. Then the corners of
his mouth turned down and he shook his head. I
disappointed him, he said. How I disappointed him.
Greatly disappointed. He touched his hand to his
heart, Victor-Hugo-style, and looking away, rambled
off about honor and professional ethics. In any event,
he let on, the assignment was over as far as I was
concerned. He'd only taken it in the first
place . . . well, if he hadn't, someone else would have.
And as he said, he didn't think they'd have to inconvenience me any more. Of course he ought to consult
his client first, but perhaps if I insisted . . . an excep-
tion . . . in the interests of professional courtesy . . . ?

I insisted. Little by little his eyelids lowered. We had
reached a point where calculation had mostly taken

over from ethics—calculation, I figured, as to how much one professional might charge another for professional courtesy—when the phone rang.

"Forgive me, *mon cher*," said J.-C. Fleurie, leaning forward to take the receiver. Then: "This is Exceptional, I'm listening."

Listen he did. It took a while, and the longer it took the more his face sagged. It had a natural sag to it, but now his dewlaps developed dewlaps and the chins seemed to multiply on his chest. Like a Slinky toy working its way down stairs, I thought. The lids closed almost entirely over his eyes, and his complexion, which had gone ruddy at moments of high oratory, now grayed steadily in the darkening light. He didn't look at me once. He focused on a ballpoint which he held upright on the desk. From time to time his fingers slid down to the base, then reversed the pen and started again from the top.

The vibrations were very bad. They got worse. Whoever he was talking to—and there were two of them—was asking questions about somebody. Apparently the somebody was me. I was there, J.-C. Fleurie said. He glanced at his watch. He swallowed. He said yes, it was serious. Yes, he agreed it was very serious. Very. And even before I heard him say Monsieur le Commissaire I was ready to agree with him.

I got up. Maybe J.-C. Fleurie misinterpreted my intentions. In any case, he was a lot quicker than I'd given him credit for. The ballpoint dropped on the desk, and in the same motion he pulled out a drawer and produced a stubby black collector's item with a snubnosed barrel. He pointed it at me. I heard the safety click. You wonder at times like that if they'd really shoot if you started out the door. But you'd hate to guess wrong. He finished the conversation with the phone in one hand and the collector's item in the other. He kept it on me when he hung up, steady-handed, and even when one of his stooges came in later, the one I'd last seen sprinting down the side street from the Boulevard St. Germain.

J.-C. Fleurie's attitude, I should say, was more of sorrow than of anger. Call it his Paris-isn't-Chicago attitude. He didn't like firearms, he said, and it offended him greatly to have to hold an illustrious colleague against his will. He didn't want me to think either that he was used to working with the Police Judiciaire or liked it any better than anyone in our profession would. As far as he was concerned, he was sure I could explain where I'd been that afternoon. As far as he was concerned, he'd be ready to let me go on my honor. But the matter was out of his hands, and there were times when one had no choice but to cooperate with the authorities. He hoped I would understand that.

"I'll tell you one thing, Monsieur Fleurie," I said. "If anything's happened to her, I'm going to twist your head off."

He stared at me, uncomprehending.

"To Binty Dove," I said.

But it wasn't to Binty that it had happened, at least as far as J.-C. Fleurie knew. It was to a member of his staff—Pierrot, the nosepicker, as it turned out. He'd been found dead, with a hole in him, in the forest of Montmorency, in the Paris suburbs.

TEN

I COULD EXPLAIN, and it could be checked out, and I did, and it was. But in between Commissaire Dedini had a field day with me, and this time there weren't even any sandwiches.

I suppose I didn't help my own cause much. Maybe we were all scum, Dedini included, but apparently there were grades of scum. It wasn't either that Pierrot the Nosepicker was a cop, albeit a private one. It was that he was French, French-born and bred and dead. Apparently that made all the difference.

"And I thought the French weren't racist," I said to Dedini.

"What are you talking about?"

"I'm talking about Jonnie Davis, Monsieur le Commissaire. Jonnison Davis, remember him? The body you fished out of the Canal St. Martin? What did you do with him, plant him six feet under and throw away the shovel? What's the difference between then and

131

now? Was it because he was only an American? Or only a nigger?"

Dedini stared across at me, over the tops of his glasses.

"You may come to regret that remark, Monsieur," he said.

"Maybe so," I retorted, "but before you start handing out the threats this time you'd better check it out first with Bernard Lascault and his friends. Or at least with Commissaire Ravier. Who knows? Maybe they'll want you to cover it up again."

In fact I think he did. In fact I know he did. But either their hands were tied this time by the fact that the crime had been committed outside of Paris, or the people who were pulling the strings had changed their signals. Because where Dedini had been effectively muzzled over Jonnie Davis, this time the opposite pressure was on him. Assuming, as I did, that he was the kind of cop who acted according to pressure.

As far as I was concerned, it was easy enough to trace and verify my whereabouts. Fleurie's stooge had placed me in the café on the Boulevard St. Germain. Theoretically it would have been possible for me to follow Pierrot from the café to Montmorency and make it back to the Exceptional Detective Agency before the end of the rugby match. But there were the people at the hotel and the two concierges in the 15th to back up my version.

The rub was that there was no way to keep Binty out of it. Fleurie's stooge had her in the café with me, and the hotel before that, and Pierrot had gone off after her. Dedini seemed particularly affronted by the notion that I could have spent twenty-four hours in a hotel with a woman and not know where she'd gone afterward. Probably it offended his sense of chivalry. Then too, whether he liked it or not, the name of Bernard Lascault kept cropping up. The apartment in the 15th was owned by Bernard Lascault, and so was the voice on the tape that answered the telephone. The relationship between Madame Dove and Monsieur Lascault, I said, was strictly business as far as I knew, which made Dedini raise his eyebrows, which made me want to yank them down. But in this regard the Law drew a blank too.

As far as I knew.

It was 11:30 P.M. before they'd finished with me. Well, but of course they'd other things to do.

Among them was a letter. It was addressed to me, on Prefecture of Police stationery, and all fancily done up, down to the "expression of my distinguished senti-ments" with which it concluded. The signature was illegible, the language officialese, and there were Arti-cles quoted and Codes cited, but the gist of the message was that I had twenty-four hours to conclude my affairs, pack my bags, and leave French soil. In other words, *persona non grata*, and if I was still on the premises twenty-four hours hence, the implication was that I'd be escorted to the nearest border and sum-marily dumped on the other side.

Actually, as Dedini pointed out, I had twenty-four hours and thirty minutes. It was only 11:30 P.M. or 23:30 as the French count it. The expulsion order wouldn't go into effect until 00:01 two days hence.

Their generosity overwhelmed me. But apparently

that wasn't Dedini's doing either. If he'd had his way, he said, I'd be spending the twenty-four and a half hours under lock and key.

"And what recourse do I have?" I asked him.

"Recourse, Monsieur?"

"I mean, I happen to be enjoying myself in Paris. I suppose there must be some sort of appeal procedure, in the land of liberty, equality, and fraternity."

He smiled at me, in a grim sort of way.

"There's only one that I know of," he said.

"What's that?"

"If you were to produce Monsieur *and* Madame Dove before the time runs out. Then perhaps this document could be torn up."

"How do you want them, Monsieur le Commissaire? With their heads on separate platters?"

For an answer he turned to one of his bloodhounds, creaking his chair, said:

"Get him out of my sight!"

Maybe I shouldn't have taken it personally. Maybe it was just his way of saying *au revoir.*

The moon was up when I came out of the Quai des Orfèvres. The Seine was a ghostly ribbon curling and snaking under the bridges and somewhere Leslie Caron had to be pirouetting on the river bank, waiting for Gene Kelly to buck-and-wing out of the mists. At that time of a Saturday night, the crowds on St. Michel, just across the river, would be elbow to elbow the width of the sidewalks, lovers and hawkers and pickpockets and panhandlers and flame swallowers, and the youth of all nations with packs strapped to their backs and guitars in one hand and hot Tunisian sandwiches in the other. Springtime in the seventies, brought to you by the makers of Paris, France, and too bad there was no place in it for me.

I was the uninvited guest, the man who came to dinner, the fifth wheel, the odd man out. I wasn't the only one either. Al Dove was in the same boat, and from what Dedini had implied, Binty was too. The boat was leaking like a sieve, and it was a case of abandon ship, every man for himself, and don't forget the loot. And people were getting killed in the ruckus. And a sap called Cage was standing by himself in the engine room with a mop and a bucket, wondering where all the water was coming from.

I walked up the quay toward the Pont St. Michel. A car eased alongside me. At first I took it for the Law— Dedini's way of proving a point—but the Law doesn't ride around in 403's any more and Peugeot quit making them some ten years back.

I stopped at the corner. So did the 403. I looked down at the driver. He looked out at me. To judge, things were going from bad to worse in the private detective business.

"Get in, Monsieur," said J.-C. Fleurie.

"Suppose I don't feel like getting in?" I said.

"Then probably you won't get in, Monsieur," said J.-C. Fleurie.

He looked like he'd swallowed his bonhomie. By a process of elimination I'd pretty much deduced who his client was, also that the party he'd been after hadn't been me, not at all, but when I tried it on him for size, he buttoned up and stared ahead through the windshield. He was shook all right. Maybe the Law was responsible for it, but it may also have been the idea that my fancy footwork that afternoon had cost him half his staff.

And in that he wouldn't have been altogether wrong.

I got in. We turned left across the Cité and the other snake of the Seine, then onto the Right Bank. I thought we were heading for his office. We passed it by though, and continued on another couple of blocks, then stopped for a red light.

"I'll have you know I'm leaving the case, Monsieur," J.-C. Fleurie said, his gaze fixed on the windshield. "This commission is my last."

"I'm sorry to hear that," I said. "Maybe we'll be able to work together . . . another time."

He didn't answer.

The light switched from red to green, but J.-C. Fleurie kept his foot on the brake.

"There's someone waiting for you inside," he said.

His eyes didn't move, but there was only one possibility: a well-lit café on the corner.

I got out.

I was expecting a man, but that only goes to show how much I'd forgotten his methods. The last time I'd seen her, she'd been aswirl in chiffon and the tawny-blond had been piled majestically on her head. Now, as she hurried through the swinging door of the café, it was down, one side of it stuck inside the turned-up collar of her coat. She wasn't wearing any makeup and she looked tired, like she'd just gotten out of bed. Maybe she had. Not that it did her any harm, and there was nothing you could say against that loyal magnolia smile.

She looked nervously past me, down the dark sidewalk. I heard the grind of gears behind me and turning, saw the 403 pull away from the curb. The small red taillights disappeared into the traffic.

"Come on, Cage," she said, linking her arm into mine.

"Where're we going, Susie? Another party?"

"Never mind. We're late."

"Late for what?"

The Giulia was only a short walk away in the Hôtel de Ville underground parking, but by way of an answer she steered me across the street and, with one last glance around us, down into the métro.

I should say in passing that I've nothing against the Paris subway, nothing particularly for it either. People who know about such things claim it's got it all over New York and London, and to judge from the number of bums who sleep on the benches and the gypsies and hippies panhandling in the corridors, there must be those who find it downright homey. On the other hand, no right-thinking Parisian would be caught alive in it, and to a lad who grew up on the shores of the Pacific and has gotten around all his life on his own four wheels, there's something pretty weird about hurtling through a hole in the ground in an over-heated tin tube jammed with thousands of sweating humanity, most of them worshippers of Allah.

Looking later on a map, I saw that the route we took described a long jagged oval, with a couple of train changes along the way at what the French call *corre-*

spondences, whereas we could have gotten there with just a short zig and a zag. For this there might have been two reasons: one, to spot and lose whoever might have tried to come along for the ride; the other, to bring us into a particular station in just the right way. But only the first occurred to me at the time. Before we got off a train, Susan Smith would squeeze my arm and rubberneck in either direction, then, satisfied, grab my hand and rush us down the passageways to the next platform. We were the last ones to get on and the first ones off, and though I don't know what she'd have done if she spotted a tail, no, there was no tail. There was just us.

We got off finally on a station platform somewhere on one of the lines that runs out of the République. By then I was completely turned around in my mind and my shirt was sticking to my back. I noticed the inevitable bum sleeping on a bench, and the same blue sign at one end with the white arrow and the white SORTIE for the exit. Only there was no yellow CORRESPON-DENCE sign to go with it. Meaning that this was a local stop, and the only way out was up to the street.

Susan Smith took my hand and led me down the platform. I realized she'd made a mistake. The handful of other passengers who'd gotten off had already passed us, heading toward the exit. In our direction was only the closed end of the station.

But she hadn't made a mistake, and the bum on the bench wasn't sleeping. In fact he wasn't on the bench any more either. When Susan Smith let go my hand, he was right behind me and that wasn't a tin cup he was holding in his hand.

"You're late, ole buddy," he said.

"Sorry about that, Al," I answered, stopping in my tracks. "I was unavoidably detained."

The train we'd come on was pulling away. I glimpsed the faces of a few people standing in the last car. The platform on the other side was empty except for a series of king-sized billboards advertising some lotion you were supposed to spread on your baby's ass.

"It doesn't matter, Cagey," said Al Dove. "We've got plenty of time. Just keep walking nice and easy. I'll tell you when to stop."

ELEVEN

ANOTHER THING I'VE LEARNED about the Paris métro: they've been modernizing it in a hurry. To a large extent this has meant getting rid of people. The old red and green trains took two men to run them; the new ones go on rubber wheels and they're computer-directed. The ticket punchers are gone, replaced by automatic magnetic readers, and the minor stations are now designed in the off-hours to be staffed by a single employee, who sits upstairs behind bars selling tickets. Of course the security may not be what it used to be, but then, so they tell me, Paris isn't Chicago, and besides, there's a convenient alarm button located on each platform for the rape victims.

This made it just about right for Al Dove, and cheaper in addition. After he sent Susan Smith on her way, he pointed me to a small boothlike affair down near the closed end of the station. It was big enough for two, three in a pinch. A small desk, a couple of wood chairs, a bulletin board with yellowed notices tacked to it, a telephone. A radiator that hissed and gurgled and put out enough heat to melt a hole in the Arctic Circle. The upper half of the booth's partitions were glass, but anyone who spotted us would have taken us for two métro featherbedders putting in their time, and whenever a new train pulled in, the artillery Al Dove held in his lap discouraged me from any notions I might have had about waving to my friends.

The artillery looked secondhand. So for that matter did Al Dove. It wasn't only the clothes or the dark stubble on his cheeks. The wind, as Bernard Lascault might have said, had gone out of his *poupe*, and the spark and movement from his eyes. They stared straight out in a kind of tired fixation that made you all the more conscious of the tics and tremors around them. It was the boxer's look when the bell's about to ring and he knows the worst is to come. Or the high roller's in the early morning, when the dice have gone cold. I'd seen it before maybe, but a long time before, back when the last of the funky summers ground to a halt on a pair of gamblers' stools in Reno, Nevada. But in those days, to a couple of underage, kicks-surfeited studs, the worst the future could hold was a helmet and a uniform. Whereas in an overheated Paris métro, a couple of decades later . . .

Well, maybe all I mean to say is that Al Dove looked like he needed the gun.

Once inside the booth, he shook me down. I was clean. My musket, as far as I know, is still gathering dust in a drawer in Santa Monica. Then we sat, just a few feet apart, on the same side of the small desk, Al

Dove with his back to the doorway and me facing him, looking at the gun, and him, and the empty tracks behind him.

The radiator cooked the rivulets which ran down my back.

And Al Dove stared at me, empty-eyed.

"It's a fucking shame," he said. "We should've been working together, baby. We always should've been. At least you can't say I never tried."

That too: an old refrain.

"Sure, Al," I said. "Like the last time we talked, you said you owed me one, that you were paying back a debt and then we'd be quits. Remember? And then your strong boy coldcocked me."

I'd have expected him to grin at me and come back with some wisecrack.

"Got to hand it to you, Cagey. I told Jonnie to put you out. Not for the count, but long enough to keep you out of our hair. He knows his business too, and Helen said you were out cold. Your skull must be as hard as Mt. Rushmore." The grin came then, but a slight and tired one. "What did you do with him? Buy him a one-way ticket to L.A.?"

What he was saying made no sense to me at first. Only then it began to—in a way I didn't like to think about.

"Secrets of the trade," I answered.

"Secrets of the trade. But you had help too, didn't you?"

"Yeah, I had help."

"I figured. Cagey's army. The minute I heard you were there, at the studio, I knew I had trouble. Hell, I knew it the minute I laid eyes on you. More trouble than I'd bargained for. I think I could have handled the rest of them, the dirty bastards. Even then. But Binty had a better idea."

"Binty's always had better ideas."

"Yeah. She sent you in, and you found the studio, and all of a sudden I had to be in two places at once. Whichever I picked, it was bound to be wrong. Helen and Bill got out in time, and I managed to get what I wanted out of the gallery, but it was too late for the rest of the stuff by the time I got to the studio. You were already gone, and Jonnie, and the joint cleaned out."

He paused. I was thinking: *but I wasn't gone, you dumb bastard, all you had to do was look upstairs.*

"How'd she do it this time, Cagey?" he went on. "With her checkbook or her cunt? Never mind. She was always pretty good with it, and you were never one to say no, were you? Like all last night, honh? Well, we've both been there, baby, and we've both been had. Only for me it's been for the last time. What about you?"

I didn't reply. All of a sudden there were too many questions running through my head. Like the one I'd asked Freddy Schwartz, which hadn't been answered. Like why Al Dove didn't know what had happened to Jonnie Davis. Like how come all I was supposed to do with Al Dove was fix him, and then she'd . . . ?

"Remember Denise?" said Al Dove softly.

The grin moved momentarily back into his eyes, then out. A train entered the station on the far side, soft-shoeing in the rubber wheels, then another one on ours. A few people got off each time, and through the window of the partition I could see them straggling toward the exit. Not a one so much as glanced at us. At first I didn't remember Denise. Then I did. Normally Denise might have made me laugh too, if a little ruefully, but I caught the reference behind Denise and the half-plea that might have gone with it, and then other images started getting in the way. Like palm trees blowing in the wind. Only they were bending now, arching their necks, and the wind starting to whistle in the fronds.

"Look Al," I said. "You went to some trouble to get me here. I doubt it was just to reminisce about old times. You're the one handling the artillery. You'd better tell me what you want."

He glanced down at his lap. His right hand clasped the gun laxly. It was only a few feet away from me. There was a chance I could have taken it from him. There was also a chance he wanted me to try.

"It's not too late for us to make a deal, Cagey."

"What kind of deal?"

"The way it stands now, nobody's got anything. We've both tried to get our hands on what the other guy has, and we've both struck out. Enough's enough. Though I must say, ole buddy, I wouldn't've thought you'd have bothered with Fleurie's man. It's not your style. Well, but I guess times have changed. Else she's got her hooks into you deeper than I'd've thought..."

The grin had come back again, a sly one, and the needle into his voice.

"I'm clean on that score," I said. "The Law . . ."

"Sure, the Law. Same old cagey Cage. I bet you've got an alibi a yard long too."

"A yard long, Al."

"A yard long. Well, let me tell it like it is, friend. We've stopped running. The rats are cornered. We're where you'd never think of looking, not in a million years . . ." Here his voice dropped almost to a whisper. ". . . but if you did . . . well, next time, Cagey, you'd better bring your army with you."

It hung there in the overheated air, the menace along with the trace of plea.

"What kind of deal, Al," I repeated.

He hesitated. Then, with a shrug:

"There are two deals, Cagey. Like I say, it's a stand-off right now. On my side, I've got one great picture and I've got Helen Raven. But no buyer. Whereas on yours, you've got two . . . well, let's say you've got two pictures. And you've the buyer and sure, you could try peddling them to her and take what you can get. Only the way I figure it, you haven't tried yet. And maybe with good reason, honh?"

The grin again.

"Have you doped it out yet, Cagey? Or only suspected? I mean, who do you think painted them? Do you think Blumenstock did? Not that anyone could tell the difference, not even an expert. They're good all right, and he had the right materials and sketches to work from. Try to prove it! Hell, she didn't even tell *me* till after we'd signed!"

The grin turned to laughter. Then the laughter went away. He was waiting for me to say something.

"The thing is, Cagey, you put it all together and they'll still be worth two million francs, and that'd be cheap the way things go these days. Three Blumenstocks for two million? It's practically a bargain! If Cookie smells a rat, not that she should, but Lascault could still do that well on the open market. At least that well. Or without Lascault! Hell, who needs Paris? There's Japan, there's the Middle East. It's America's revenge, baby! What's more . . ."

He went on with it, working himself up as he went. I let him go. I watched him while he talked and I heard the words, but my mind was heating up in a hurry inside. *He's got some property that belongs to us*, she'd said. It hadn't even occurred to me that the property was split, and she hadn't seen fit to tell me. And why was that? Turn it around as I might, I could only come up with one answer: she didn't want me to know. *Just find him, fix him,* she'd said, *and I'll take care of it then.* And why didn't she want me to know? *He's scared to death of you*, she'd said. *Kiss me*, she'd said. *Kiss me again.*

Al Dove was laying it on me now, and I heard him and I didn't hear. Because the palms were bending and scrunching their necks and the storm rolling toward them, the waves rising and crashing, the lightning screeching across the bloody sky like chalk on a giant blackboard. And Al Dove was telling me that together we could do it. He knew where the pictures were as well as I did now. Lascault's place in L'Isle-Adam, where else? That's where Fleurie's man had been headed. He'd go himself, now that he knew where, only he didn't want to share the same fate. But together, the two of us, sure we could pull it off. Because the Blumenstock setup was intact, that was the beauty of it. They'd ripped off the rest of his operation, had they? Well, they were welcome to it. But three pictures for two million or more, and Lascault could be brought around once it was a *fait accompli*, and besides, what was there that said we had to stop at three when nobody knew how many there were? What was to keep people from accepting five, or eight, or ten, if it was organized right? Because there was room in it for Cage, plenty of room. Because his deal with Helen Raven and Rillington was fifty percent of the proceeds but he'd cut them to a third, that was no problem, didn't a third of something beat a half of nothing?

It was my fourth offer. The first two had fallen by the wayside. The last two were a hell of a recommendation for holy matrimony.

The storm died down inside. Down, say, to a whisper, soft and warm and licking at my ear. *Kiss me*, the whisper said. *Kiss me again.*

I was sweating all over. He was staring at me. I saw the knuckles of his gun hand stiffen and whiten.

"Geezus, Cagey," he said in a strained voice, "you never forget, do you."

In hindsight, I realize that he was talking about something else, something that went back in time almost as far as Denise. Call it the real bone of contention between us. But on the spot, all I said was:

"What's the other deal, Al?"

He'd been watching me, ramrod stiff. Then all of a sudden, and all together, the muscles of his head and body seemed to let go. His face, his neck, his shoulders. It was like he'd put the last of his chips on the come line and let fly, and thrown a pair of eyes again just like he'd known he would secretly. All at once he gave up, and the air went out of the pumpkin.

"All right," he said tonelessly. "I'm tap city, Cagey. It's yours. All I want is a fair stake, and then I'll lay it in your lap, the whole package: the portrait, Helen Raven, Rillington. Then you can play it like you want to. You'll have to do your own negotiating with them, but it shouldn't be hard. All Helen really wants is revenge on Cookie Lascault, and Rillington'll do whatever she tells him to."

Another train rolled into the station, the last one as it turned out. But no one got on and no one got off, and if there was anyone else on the platform besides us, I didn't notice.

"How much is a fair stake, Al?" I said.

"I figure ten percent of the original deal I had worked out. That's two hundred thousand francs, and if you play it right, two hundred thou could be a lot less than ten percent. If I have to, I'll take half in cash and half in a note. The only thing is: I want it fast. I'll give you till tomorrow night. No more. Otherwise . . ."

He paused.

"Otherwise what?" I said.

But all I got for an answer was a staccato laugh and: "Hell, baby, some day you ought to try living on the run with a bitch like that."

He glanced at his watch. Tomorrow—or today—was Sunday, but he figured Lascault still ought to be able to come up with that kind of cash. He'd meet me at the same place, at ten o'clock that night. I was to bring the money, alone. Then he'd tell me where to go.

He glanced at his watch again. Something seemed to revive him momentarily, the idea maybe that, because he'd said it, that was how it was going to happen. Then with a brief grin he placed the gun on the little desk between us.

It lay there.

"Your move, baby. Only remember: I know where they are and you don't."

Maybe so, but he'd given me a pretty good idea. And in hindsight, I'd have to say he meant to.

I was looking at him and the empty tracks behind him. Someone moved into the gap between. For a split second it might have been my move at that, but the split second came and went and then Helen Raven was standing in the doorway behind him, a gun in her hand. It was pointed at the back of Al Dove's head.

How much she'd heard I didn't know. Enough in any case.

"You're selling cheap, aren't you, Al," she said. It came out a statement, not a question. He started, but she jammed the barrel end hard into his neck. "If you turn around, you bastard, I'll blow your head off. You!" she snapped at me. "Very carefully now. I want you to brush that gun off the desk and onto the floor. Don't try to pick it up."

"Wait a minute, Professor," I said. "Guns that are brushed onto the floor have a way of going off. I . . ."

"*You shut up!*" she shrilled at me. You could feel the suppressed hysteria oozing out of her pores and Al Dove's pupils went large in their sockets. "*You do what I tell you to do! NOW!*"

I did, very carefully. The artillery clattered at my feet. Then it lay still.

She told Al Dove to push forward in his chair. He

did, until we were sitting knee to knee, at which she
moved inside the booth and covered us both.

"Two hundred thousand francs," she said, the
words bursting scornfully out of her. "That's cheap,
Al. Isn't that cheap? What wouldn't you sell for two
hundred thousand francs? And only half of it in cash.
After all I've been through, that's what it comes down
to. To be sold out for two hundred thousand francs by
a cheap gangster."

"Wait a minute, Helen, you've . . ."

"*Shut up!*" The command shrilled again in the small
booth. "*Stand up, Al!*"

He stood up. His face, pale and tense, loomed over
me. I could see the sweat bubbling on his forehead. He
looked like he thought he was going to check out any
second.

"I've had enough of your schemes, your sweet talk,
your reassurances! If you're so damn clever, how come
you let *me* follow you here? You said the portrait alone
would be worth half a million, didn't you? Half a
million minimum, isn't that what you said? Well suppose I decide I won't sell it at *any* price? Suppose that's
my price: *no* price! Then what the hell do I need you
for?"

"You're crazy!" he shouted, half-turning his head.
"They'll chew you up and spit you out! Don't be a
damn fool, Helen, you'll get nothing! You'll . . ."

"*SHUT UP, GOD DAMN YOU!*"

It was alarm time in the cockpits of hell. The boiler
was about to blow. The gongs were going off and the
red lights flashing, the dials spinning and the voices of

panic bleeping out of control. It was time to bail out . . .
for Alan Dove, ex-courtier, and for B. F. Cage as well.

But just then, without warning, the lights went out.
It happened first on the far platform, then on ours.
Click followed by *click*, and the station plunged into
darkness.

It threw her, just for a second. I'd already dug my
chair into the wall. Now I thrust off, driving for the
doorway. Only Al Dove had the opposite reflex. He
stooped, ducking either from her or for the gun. My
head, then my shoulder, slammed into him, flinging
him back, and the cannon went off between us even as
we catapulted into her. I took the blast of it right in the
eyes and somewhere behind me a thousand sheets of
glass shattered into a million or more small pieces.
Then the three of us exploded out of the booth in a
burst of pinwheeling bodies, like somebody had flung
a grenade among us, and something carved my legs
out from under me neatly and plunged me forward,
smashing my face into the stone of the platform. I
scraped and slid painfully toward the edge, and I saw
the stars you're supposed to see all right, only they had
jagged edges and they pulsed and tore in time to my
blood beat, and a herd of heavenly horses went charging across my skull and down the platform, racing for
the last train.

Only the last train had gone. And there weren't any
horses, only two ghostly shapes swaying and stagger-
ing to their feet on a cosmic platform a couple of
light-years off. Something had gone screwy with my
vision. It was like the whole dark station was flashing in
light but the two of them were ghosts, like after-images

or white blurs on a negative. I saw Al Dove wobbling near the booth. His hands seemed to be raised above his head. A long way away I heard his voice telling her not to be crazy, telling her she'd never get away with it alone, telling her the station was already locked, that even if she killed us both she'd never get out of the fucking station. Even then, half-stunned and with the panic squeezing his larynx, he was trying to make a deal. But the Professor was beyond listening. I'd seen her scabbling on the platform, I'd seen her come up with the gun. She held it out in front of her, in both hands, and if the rest of her was teetering like a drunken tightrope walker, the gun was clenched stiff. She backed off a couple of steps. Then she fired: once, twice, three times, her body jumping each time, and turned, and ran down the platform in the direction of the darkened exit, and the echoes of the blasts were drowned out by Al Dove's screaming.

TWELVE

I TASTED BLOOD. It was trickling down from my nose. I got to my feet. From somewhere came a dim light, but I didn't have to wait for my eyes to adjust to it to find Al Dove.

He was shaking with shock and screaming his bloody head off. He was convinced he was going to croak any second, and even if he didn't Helen Raven would be back to finish us off. The only recourse was the tunnel. We had to get into the tunnel before she came back. He tried to stand up, but cried out instead and sank backwards onto a bench and started begging me to finish him off, please Jesus God Cagey to get the gun and put him out of his misery. Whereupon it took all my strength to hold him to the bench, because Helen was going to be back any second, the entrance would be locked, there was no other way out, she'd shoot us down like rats in a trap if we didn't get into the fucking tunnel.

As it happened, he was wrong on both counts: Helen Raven wasn't coming back, and he wasn't about to croak. As near as I could tell, two of her bullets had missed altogether. The third had pierced his left breast but high, almost at the armpit, and it had come out under his shoulder blade. Or most of it. There wasn't much blood. It could have nicked bone on the way through and he'd need to see a doctor, but I was pretty sure he'd live all right.

If, that is, he didn't die of fright first.

Because the fear was in him, along with that end-of-the-road sobbing and blubbering and remorse which is one of the sorrier spectacles, even in a world short on heroics. To understand it, you'd probably have to go back before the cocky young guinea I'd first known, back to the altar boy lighting candles in St. Geronimo's in downtown San Berdoo.

But like I say, I can't take you that far, and come to think of it, he himself stopped short of calling for a priest, that night there in the métro.

Though maybe that was because he got his ole buddy Cage to hear his last confession.

Roll it back then, a couple of decades and then some, to where I came in. I've called it the last of the funky summers, and it was a pretty weird time. Another war was starting up, people said it was the beginning of Big Three, but to those of us who were eligible to fight it or almost, it was bugoutsville, fuck it, every man for himself. As far as Mrs. Cage's boy was concerned, I took off the day after my junior year in high school, leaving a good-by note pinned to the Post Toasties. I worked my way south, the length of the great and sovereign state of California. I got laid in Pershing Square, got the crap pounded out of me in Echo Park, and thumbed my way east across the desert with nothing in my wallet but a pack of safes and two draft cards, one of which said eighteen, the other twenty-one, and both of them fake. In Kingman, Arizona, I signed on with a pipeline crew. I worked, ate, slept, and gambled with a bunch of oversized aztecs and apaches until I had two hundred and fifty bucks clear. Then I headed some ninety miles up the road, to Paradise.

Paradise? Well, they called it Vegas, too. Maybe the Flamingo had only just gone up, and surely nobody in town had even heard of Howard Hughes, but to a red-blooded youth with cash money in his jeans, it was Baghdad, Gomorrah, and the Leaning Tower of Pisa all rolled into one. The neon popped your eyeballs. You could eat your fill of steak for a couple of bucks and see a show at the same time. They had these cute little dealers with lacquered fingernails sharp enough to cut the Ace of Spades in two, and those who weren't dealing came around every half hour or so with drinks on the house. Plus slot machines in every head, metal dollars instead of paper, and everybody talking about some old stiff too drunk to walk who'd run $50 into $13,000 at the Golden Nugget the night before.

I took the Governor's Suite in the biggest hotel on Fremont, cash on the barrelhead. Then I decked myself out like Napoleon on the eve of Austerlitz and set out to parlay Cage's Sure-Thing Blackjack System into a trip to Mexico or Rio or pretty much anywhere south of Yakima, Washington, where they had hot and cold running maids and champagne in the spigots.

About eighteen hours and maybe thirty-six white lightnings later, I remember the cute little dealer tapping her fingernail on the felt to see if I was up. I remember fumbling through my pockets and coming up with what was left of a one-way bus ticket to nowhere. I remember that the cute little dealer's lips were as red as her fingernails and that she had black eyes and black shiny hair. And that's the last thing I remember until I woke up the next morning, if it was morning, dry-mouthed and sick-bellied, on the deep pile rug of the Governor's Suite, with this dude who'd been playing next to me konked out on His Excellency's bed.

We introduced ourselves. Al, meet B. F. Cage. Cagey, meet Al Dovici, in cowboy boots and chinos.

We inventoried our remaining assets. These consisted of our clothes and my bus ticket. We went down to the depot and traded in what was left of the bus ticket for a couple of platters of scrambled eggs and hashed browns. But then we were tapped out and walking the streets, touchy as a pair of ovulating broads and itching all over from that big gnawing get-even gambler's feeling. The sickness is short, and no junkie ever had it worse.

Until we ran into Denise.

Actually she was a schoolteacher on vacation, and she wasn't half bad. She came from somewhere in Wisconsin. She drove one of those coffee-grinder '47 Fords. She fed us and shared her motel room with us and just about everything else except her hoard. She gave us a couple of bucks a day for walking-around money. It would last us maybe fifteen minutes and then we'd come begging, but she said she wasn't about to let a couple of underage losers blow her year's savings. So mostly we watched her, at roulette, and in between spins of the wheel we took turns balling her. But after a few days of balling and watching, the itch was driving us clean out of our sockets.

Then she decided to take a day off, if it was okay with us. It was okay with us. We loaded the back of the Ford with as much beer as it could hold and drove down to Lake Mead. It's a beautiful spot, Lake Mead, even if it is man-made, and Boulder Dam holds it all together. We swam, and baked in the sun, and played grabass in the shallow water, and drank beer, swam some more, drank some more, and when we ran out of beer all three of us fell asleep.

Except for Al and me.

He looked at me, and I looked at him.

"C'mon Cagey," he said. "It's bug-out time."

We sold the Ford to a moon-faced aztec in Vegas who would have paid you 25 percent of value for your town fire engine. Then we got on a bus for Reno, where Al said the real action was, and where the first and last of the funky summers came to an abrupt halt, about six A.M. one late August morning.

I remember it well. We'd had our run. We'd doubled our stake, then doubled the doubled, but before you could say eighter from Decatur, the dice went stone-age cold in our hands. I remember him turning away from the table, red-eyed, and feeling not the sickness any more, just done in, wasted, and him laying it on me:

"Fuck it, Cagey. Let's join the fucking army and get it over with."

We had to lie about our age, but all the recruiters did in those cannon-fodder days was count your eyes. We went through basic training together and a couple of months later the two of us and a few thousand other young braves were paddling west across the dark and deep Pacific to save the free world.

Only Al Dovici managed to get off in Japan. How I never quite knew at the time, only that it was one of those now-you-see-me-now-you-don't deals, because one morning he was present and accounted for in the replacement company and the next, another sorry stiff was standing in his place. In between there'd been an all-night poker game. Oh yes, and the other sorry stiff was me. I had a one-way ticket to a place called Kunuri, Korea, and when I got there a padded Chinaman on horseback punched me the rest of the way through to Prison Camp Number Five up at Pyoktong, and if it was too long a walk to get there for Christmas, I had the next one and the one after to make up for it.

I used to think about him in the bad times. I could see the pair of dice in his palm, hear him sweet-talking them. I used to wonder what would have happened if one of those snake eyes had rolled over on its back and come up a six. Or if the dealer with the red fingernails had slipped me an ace to go with my king instead of a trey. Or if I'd read William Shakespeare in high school instead of Captain Marvel. Then Al would butt in in my mind, in the middle of one of those bullshit conversations we'd had about what we were going to do after the war, saying: *A private eye? Geezus, Cagey, you must be out of your mind!* Because he'd had us opening up the biggest chain of cathouses the West Coast had ever seen, all the way from Puget Sound to Chula Vista. And I'd wonder if he'd organized Yokohama for starters. But then the day came when his hitch would have been up, mine too, and after that I stopped thinking about him as much as I could, and about mostly everything.

I ran into him again in San Francisco, late in 1953. I'd been all over the country, courtesy of the U.S. Army, telling my ugly story about the Communist statements I'd signed as far east as Washington, D.C., and to no one under the rank of major. It was still up for grabs whether they were going to let me go or put me to making little rocks out of big for the next ten years or so. In the end they chose the first solution, but under conditions "other than honorable," which meant among other things that I never could get that investigator's license I hankered after. Or so I thought then, and by the time I found out who to pay off, I no longer gave a damn.

In any case, by 1953 Al Dove was already running a string of hookers in and out of the Broadway saloons. Later on he traded the girls in for cars, then the cars for dope, the dope for real estate, the real estate finally for art, but the scenario was always the same: the action was always terrific, the mob was involved somewhere, and there was always plenty of room in it for his ole buddy Cage.

Only his ole buddy Cage never forgot, did he?

No, probably he didn't. Not even when he finally got his own thing together. Not certainly after that boozy reunion on Broadway in San Francisco, 1953, when Al Dove told him his version of what had happened in Japan.

There'd been a poker game all right in the replacement company, an all-nighter, and for the first and maybe only time in his life Al Dove had gotten out at the right time. He'd taken them all, but none more than a certain sergeant whom he'd cleaned right down to his socks, and then some. When the time came to settle up, he was holding a fistful of the sergeant's markers. This had created quite a ticklish problem. To which, however, there was one simple solution. The sergeant had finally agreed. In exchange for the markers, he simply struck the name of Dovici from a certain roster. What Al hadn't realized, he said, was that somebody else was going to have to go in his place, and by the time he found out that the somebody was his ole buddy Cage, they'd already pulled up the anchor and thrown away the gangplank.

No, I guess I never forgot. Not even a couple of decades later in the Paris métro, when the real story came pouring out.

Actually, his setup for that night had been just as simple. The métro shuts down a little after one A.M. Shortly after the passage of the last train, the station attendant makes his final rounds, wakes up the bums, turns off the lights, then closes and chains the metal grilles across the entrance and snaps shut the padlocks and abandons the joint to the rats. Al Dove had paid the attendant to keep the grilles open till he came out. The way he'd had it figured, his parley with his ole buddy Cage could have taken one of several turns, but no matter what happened he'd have his escape route, and by the time I found mine he'd have been long gone.

What is it they say about history repeating itself?

Only this time it had blown. This time Helen Raven held the markers, and he hadn't planned on her showing up to collect, much less leaving him with a hole in his shoulder. Maybe you could say he'd been there before, in spots as tight and tighter, and had managed to wriggle through. But this time he had no wriggle left, only a lot of whimper and cower, plus a confession the size of the Matterhorn weighing on his brain.

First though, armed with his cannon and my matches, I left him and went up the exit stairs. If the Professor was hiding in a broom closet, she didn't come out. The ticket booth was empty, the door to it locked, and so was every other door I found. I vaulted over the turnstiles and came up against the first of two grilles, one at the bottom of the steps up to the street, the other at the top. Both were padlocked. It wasn't hard to imagine the attendant's reaction when the Professor changed his instructions. I saw the gray glow of the upstairs world through the grilles, heard the sporadic sounds of traffic. Maybe I could have shot our way out, but that's a trickier business than they make it out in the movies, and the last thing I wanted right then was company, particularly in uniform.

Finally I made my way back down to the platform.

The light was better there. I realized that it came from the single bulbs strung at intervals through the tunnels. Al Dove was slumped forward on the bench. His shirt was damp but more from sweat, I judged, than blood. I tore the sleeve of it off his good side and made a makeshift bandage with it, lit one of his cigarettes for him, then went to the booth. It wasn't my day for telephones though. I didn't get so much as a bleep out of the receiver, and no combination of numbers I tried produced a dial tone. The line was dead. The choice, as far as I could see, came down then to trying to shoot off the padlocks or waiting till the system opened up again in the early morning.

But Al Dove had another idea.

I checked it out on the métro map with one of my last matches. It looked feasible enough.

"All right," I said, coming back to where he was sitting, "let's get to going. We've got some walking to do."

"Who? Me?"

He laughed—a short sound that ended up in a cough. He shook his head. He said he couldn't make it. There'd be some acrobatics at the end, even if he got that far he couldn't handle the acrobatics. And what for anyway? What the hell for? He was tired of running. If Helen Raven didn't get him, he had some friends back in California who would, sooner or later. He was washed up and hurting, and all he wanted was for me to leave him the gun in case Helen Raven came back.

I told him that was so much bullshit. He may have been hurting, but he wasn't about to croak. I told him

Helen Raven wasn't coming back. I told him I thought he might still have a crack at his payoff, at least the cash part. I told him I could carry him out if need be.

But he wasn't having any of it. And then, all of a sudden, it came gushing out of him, punctuated by sobbing and coughing: that ugly spew of true confession that people think is all the world needs to set it right. The gist of it was that he'd lied to me all those years before. He'd been in the poker game all right, and he'd cleaned up, but when the sergeant agreed to the deal, he'd insisted on a substitute, somebody with the same MOS. The sergeant had had a body count to fill, he hadn't cared who he filled it with as long as the numbers came out right. And Al Dove had given him . . .

. . . his ole buddy Cage.

"I did it as a joke, Cagey!" he whined at me. "I swear! I thought it was just a joke! Geezus Christ, I even remember the son of a bitch's name! Sergeant Kiminy! I can't forget it! Sergeant Francis Fucking Kiminy!"

He'd started to shiver. I put my raincoat around him. I told him it was all right, and hearing myself say it, I guessed that it was. Either it had happened too long ago, or somehow I'd known all along. Oh, I was a regular old mother to him.

But I couldn't budge him.

"Get going, Cagey," he said finally. "Stick one in her for me." Then, in a hoarse whisper: "Just leave me the fucking gun."

I thought about that a moment. I assumed his her and the one I was going after were different, but in hindsight I was wrong about that. But right about the gun. I figured he wouldn't shoot me if I gave it to him. He didn't. I was pretty sure he wouldn't shoot himself either.

I went into the tunnel. The last thing I heard from him was a panicky shout:

"Come back, Cagey! Geezus Christ, you can't leave me here to die!"

I suppose, though, that it's a testament to something or other about the Al Doves of this world that when the police finally showed up, all they found were the padlocks blasted off the grilles up near the street and the two gates ajar.

THIRTEEN

A FEW STATIONS down the line, the métro came out of
the ground and crossed the Seine on a bridge. It was
no big deal to walk it, and I wouldn't even mention it if
it weren't for my furry little enemies. The tunnel was
full of them, and those I didn't see I invented. I went
from tie to tie, plagued by the idea of stepping on one.
The further I went the more it worked me over, and I
fought it off like a kid in the dark telling himself there
are no rats, there are no rats, while my body over-
heated like an engine racing in first gear and the smell
of me brought them squeezing through the chinks and
cracks.

I guess it's a dumb enough phobia for a grown man.
I mean, you know they're there. Some say the underground population of Paris, France, is several times
larger than the human Besides, hadn't there been that

time in my life, on the far side of the globe, when we'd hunted and roasted them, a gaunt band of scarecrows armed with sticks and bare hands?

Sure, there'd been that time.

Still, when the tracks finally started climbing in a big slow leftward curve, I broke into a run. And when I smelled the cool night air, saw the gray glow of the Paris sky, I felt like I was coming out of the bowels of hell all right, but a hell made up of leaping scurrying creatures no bigger than your foot, with eyes of solid pupil and bodies cringing with fear and appetite.

I climbed onto a narrow ledge. It led in turn to a platform. Just after the tracks came out aboveground was another station, the last one before the river. Down below was the Right-Bank expressway, beyond it the Seine.

I found myself gulping air. I let it wash over me. My legs were trembling—those quirky little uncontrollable jumps just under the skin, and I held onto the balustrade, watching the Seine and the sparse lights of the cars, until they went away.

The moon had long since set. I was well up the river from the center of town, and any minute, it seemed to me, the sky would start to brighten. But my watch said only 2:45 A.M.

I had some phone calls to make.

I went over the parapet and edged along the outside ledge until I reached the exit staircase, a spidery column that descended out of the station and doubled back on itself to the quays below. Then I worked my way down the outside of it, hand under hand and foot under foot, until I could jump back down among the living.

The living, though, were largely asleep. I finally found a pay phone on the quays, but when I reached into my pockets for change, I came up empty-handed. Helped out by a red light, I stopped an empty cab. He was going home, emergency or not, and it wasn't till I stuffed a hundred-franc bill into his meter that I got him to dig into his change purse and come up with half a dozen twenty-centime pieces. At that the exchange rate must have impressed him, because he hung around while I called and later, after a detour to a café near the Gare de Lyon, he dropped me off at the Hôtel de Ville underground garage where I changed into the Giulia.

I tried twice to get the message through to Dedini. But the commissaire, it turned out, didn't work all the time after all. In fact it being Sunday, there was every chance he couldn't be reached till Monday. I started to tell my story to the duty officer at Police Secours, but he broke in on me, telling me he was transferring me to the Police Judiciaire, and then somewhere between Police Secours and the Police Judiciaire the damn line went dead in my ear. The second time around I started shouting into the mouthpiece even as the same clown answered. Strangely enough, it worked. I told him they'd better get hold of the commissaire in a hurry, that half the package was ready for delivery, that Alan Dove was currently locked in a métro station with a hole in his shoulder and that if they didn't get moving he could bleed to death. I gave him the location, and then he came back on calmly, asking me what the name was please?

"DOVE!" I exploded into the phone. "D-O-V-E. He's the man you're supposed to be looking for!"

No, but he had that much. It was my name he wanted.

"CAGE!" I shouted. "C-A-G-E."

"Would you mind spelling that please?"

I laughed, more in sorrow than in anger. I spelled it for him again, slowly, in French. But when he started getting personal, like asking where I was calling from, I broke the connection. The last thing I wanted, on my last day in Paris, was the company of the Law.

With the cabbie's remaining two coins I reached . . . Bernard Lascault's taped voice. I hung up and banged the metal box with my fist, which brought a small cascade of change into the return slot. Not that it did me any good. There was no way you could call outside Paris on that phone, not with all the twenty-centime pieces in the world.

Or so the cabbie informed me. He was a big-bellied Frenchman, with a red face and a squashed nose. He'd been leaning against his car, cleaning his fingernails with a crimped matchstick, while I tried to dial the third number. He asked me where I was calling. I said L'Isle-Adam. He said I'd never get L'Isle-Adam on a blue phone. I looked at the one I'd been using. It was blue all right. I asked him where I could find a red or a yellow or just a plain old black one.

He thought it over. Then with a belch and a heavy sigh, he told me to get in, and we found the open café near the Gare de Lyon, where another hundred francs set him up behind a flagon of café red and got me the use of the patron's instrument.

The connection went through before the second ring. What's more, there was no trace of sleep in the voice that answered. Nor, for that matter, was it taped.

"This is Bernard Lascault," said Bernard Lascault, live.

"Welcome back, Mr. Lascault," I said. "And this is Cage, remember me? Your friendly neighborhood investigator? I'm sorry to bother you in the middle of the night, but I'm trying to reach Mrs. Dove."

"Where did you get this number?" he asked suspiciously.

"Oh, my fairy godmother gave it to me." Which was true, in a way. It was the first of the numbers La Ducrot had punched out that day in her office. "But about Mrs. Dove, Mr. Lascault. I'm trying to contact her. It's pretty urgent."

"I'm afraid I wouldn't know how to help you."

"You wouldn't?"

"No, I wouldn't. Where are you calling from?"

"Never mind about that. But it's pretty peculiar, isn't it? Mrs. Dove was staying with you, wasn't she? In your apartment in town? I'm not the only one who knows about that, by the way. The police do too. And she told me that's where she'd be. As of this afternoon— yesterday afternoon, that is—that's what she told me Only she's not there."

"I   "

"But you wouldn't know about that either, would you?"

"Let me tell you something. You've been meddling in matters that don't concern you. I don't believe I'm the first to have told you that either, but you seem to forget it as soon as you've heard it. That's a dangerous habit. Even the most patient people lose their patience. If I were you . . ."

"But you're not me," I interrupted. "And before you start handing out advice, you should check it first with Mrs. Dove. Anyway, maybe I'd like to stop meddling and maybe I wouldn't, but it's gone beyond that. Beyond patience too. People have started shooting, in case you haven't heard, and somebody I know is walking around with a twenty-four-hour expulsion notice in his pocket. But I suppose you wouldn't know anything about that either, would you?"

"No, I wouldn't," he said, his voice rising. "In point of fact, I just got back this evening."

"Yeah, I heard you were out of town." I glanced at the clock behind the bar. It would have been evening in New York and cocktail hour on the West Coast. "Now don't tell me, let me guess. I bet you've been visiting your farflung enterprises. Like your L.A. branch? Tell me, how are things in sunny California?"

He didn't answer. But suddenly his absence those last few days began to make sense.

"I didn't think you'd stoop so low," I said. "I mean, in the people you associate with. I thought you preferred to deal through courtiers."

"That doesn't concern you. Not in the slightest. I've told you before. The affair is closed."

"All right," I said. "Then just give Mrs. Dove a

message for me. Like the next time you happen to run
into her." My voice slowed down to a walk. "Tell her
I've found her property. All of it."

There was silence at the other end of the line, followed by some kind of commotion, followed by silence
again.

I thought he might have hung up on me.

But then, small-voiced:

"Is that you, Cagey?"

"None other," I answered, going tight inside.

"Are you all right?"

"Oh, not so bad. I got scraped up a little and my face
isn't too pretty, but you should've seen the other guy.
How about you?"

"I was so scared, Cagey. Where're you calling from?"

"Let me see." I gazed around the café. "I think it's a
place called Paris."

She didn't laugh. She didn't say anything.

"The other guy was Al, Binty," I said.

By this time the conversation had gone distinctly one
way.

"I found him for you," I said. "Or—not that it matters—he found me. Isn't that what you wanted me to
do?"

"What did you do to him?" she said finally. There
was a trace of dread in her voice, more than a trace, but
in hindsight that could have been taken in opposite
ways.

"Oh, nothing much really," I answered. "We talked
over old times."

"Is he with you now?"

"No. In fact the last I saw of him, he had a small hole in him. About the size of a dime. But I expect he'll pull through."

"Where is he?"

"I imagine by now the Law's got him."

"The police?"

"Don't worry, they'll take good care of him. The only trouble is there's another stiff they can't do anything for, fellow by the name of Pierrot. Worked for a detective agency, wouldn't you know? By a queer coincidence, they found him in the Montmorency forest. That's not far from where you are, is it? Stranger still, it turns out he was one of the tails in that café on the Boulevard St. Germain. Remember?"

"God," she said. But there wasn't much conviction in it. Then, huskily: "Did you kill him, Cagey?'

"No. Did you?"

It mightn't have done much for her in court, but there was a kind of honesty at that . . . in her silence.

"I've also located that missing property you wanted," I went on. "That is, if you and Bernard are still interested in it. You are, aren't you?"

I paused, waiting for a reaction. I mean, it's not the money that counts, but you'd like a little recognition now and then.

"Yes," she answered finally. "We are. Where is it?"

"I'm afraid that's going to cost you some."

"How much?"

"Oh, say two hundred thousand francs. Cash And then you'll have to do your own negotiating."

"Who with?"

"With Helen Raven, I expect. The only trouble with that is . . . well, Helen's in a sort of nasty mood these days. For one thing, somebody's got some of her property too. Or what she thinks is hers."

Another pause. Then:

"Cagey, I think we'd better talk."

"Yeah, good idea. When and where? Do you want me to come out there?"

"Out here? No, not out here. What about your hotel?"

It was a hell of a thing. Just the day before we'd been death-do-us-part lovers and now we were arguing about where to meet. But I didn't like the idea of the hotel any better than she liked L'Isle-Adam.

I suggested Lascault's apartment over in the 15th. I told her I could be there in half an hour.

For some reason, this agitated her no end.

"*Half an hour?* You must be out of your mind, darling! It's the middle of the night!"

"Oh? Well, so it is. I must have forgotten. Funny thing, but I feel fresh as a daisy."

I hadn't realized that I'd interrupted her beauty sleep. I hadn't realized either—I guess because I didn't want to—that every time she dropped her end of the dialogue, it was to check her lines with her friend Bernard. And anybody else who happened to have dropped by.

"I'll tell you what," she said, coming back on. "Don't get the wrong idea, my darling, but I think we could both use a few hours' sleep. Me at least. Why don't we meet there in the morning? I'll get there as fast as I can. Is nine o'clock all right? Can you be there at nine?"

"Any time you say."

"And Cagey . . . are you still there, Cagey?"

"Sure. I'm right here."

"Don't misunderstand. I love you, my man. It's just that . . ."

She let it hang there. I finished it for her.

"I get it, Binty. You mean that the wind's died down."

"What?"

"Never mind."

"Okay. I'll explain everything in the morning. I'll be there. Sleep well, my darling."

She kissed me over the phone. So she said. I hung up, and after checking the timer he'd set when I began the call, the patron started to make me change.

I told him to keep it.

The cabbie had worked his way about halfway through the wine. I helped him finish it. On the first swallow I thought I could still taste the peasant feet that had stomped the grapes, but it got better as it went, and the second flagon was a big improvement over the first.

I got some sleep. More, I imagine, than she did. First, though, the Giulia and I made a short reconnaissance run. *Not in a million years*, Al Dove had said, but I knew my man, and the location of the métro station helped turn a hunch into a shrewd conclusion. One, moreover, I like to think he wanted me to reach.

They'd run out of places to hide all right.

Then we drove slowly back to the Seine, and across,

and up the Left-Bank quays with only the blinking yellow traffic lights for company. We went past the Institute and the Mint, ghostly shapes in the night, past the Invalides and the Eiffel, until these gave way in turn to the Front de Seine development and the Hilton and the rest of what passes for twentieth-century Paris.

The whole city seemed to float by in a gray and untroubled sleep. Millions of people sleeping in stacks, and horizontal rows. It was contagious. When we got to our destination, we made one slow pass up the block. The trees were blurred shadows in the sparse light, the façades were totally dark. We circled around and came back in, then tucked into a space some two cars in from the corner. Then I slumped down in my seat, gave the Giulia a soft chorus of "*Auprès de Ma Blonde*," pulled my beret over my eyes, and the next sound we heard was the garbage truck making its rounds shortly after dawn.

FOURTEEN

My watch said 7:32. At 7:34 the Mercedes slid through my side mirror, followed by the Renault van. A little further on, the garbage truck blocked the street, and the natives in orange vests who were loading it up seemed in no particular hurry. At least, that is, until the driver of the Mercedes got out. From my vantage point I couldn't see what he did, but he must have been a pretty persuasive fellow. The spades jumped onto the side rear platforms like they'd been goosed, and the garbage truck trundled to the end of the block and disappeared around the corner.

The Mercedes eased into a slot about halfway down. The Renault van stayed double-parked. Four people got out of the Mercedes and entered Lascault's building. Two were male, one female, and the fourth an immense black specimen with a tattersall cap on his head who looked like he could have picked his teeth with Jonnie Davis.

Mrs. Al Dove and friends, and it looked to me like the Americans had landed again.

You'd have thought they might have worried about what people would say. About all that uncollected garbage on the sidewalk, for one thing. Or about their taking their gorilla inside without a leash. Or about picking a Sunday morning to do their moving. But none of these things seemed to cause them the slightest concern. A few minutes later the two white men emerged from the front door struggling with a large flat oblong object about as tall as them and half again as long. Call it a painting and you wouldn't be far off. The gorilla followed them out with another one of about the same size tucked under his arm. By this time the driver of the Renault van had the rear doors open. They slid the pictures inside, and the driver closed and locked the doors with a key.

Then Binty Dove came out of the building. She'd changed her clothes from the day before, except for the ivory-colored raincoat. She looked about ready for church. Otherwise, murder hadn't changed her a bit. She stood on the sidewalk with her back to me, conferring with her troops, while the sun made shadows on the façades and the budding trees emerged tall and straight.

Then the driver got into the Renault van and Binty, after a glance up and down the sidewalk in either direction, walked into the street and climbed in on the passenger's side. The three heavies watched from the sidewalk until the van had turned the corner, then turned themselves and single-filed into the building.

I hoped they'd at least brought a deck of cards, because it looked like they had a long wait in front of them. But I didn't stick around to find out.

At that I almost blew them coming out of Paris. A gorgeous day was in the making, the sky a shade of blue you only see in postcards and movies, with a scattering of low white puffball clouds for comic relief. The air was so soft as to turn the hardest heart to reveries of picnics and nymphs and carousing in the bushes. In short: a city dweller's dream and a traffic cop's nightmare. Within a couple of hours every road leading out of the city would be choked and the Boulevard Périphérique a solid circle of inching vehicles. Horns would be blowing, tempers flying, radiators boiling over. Already at eight you had premonitions of it, in the no-quarter tactics of the early birds rushing to get out while the getting was good.

To go to L'Isle-Adam, you quit the autoroute in St. Denis and follow the Nationale 1 out toward Montmorency. The Renault van left the autoroute all right, but when we got to where the N1 forks into the N16, he veered right out of the turn lane. I went after him, but out of the straight-ahead lanes and only by stepping on a solid white line and a couple of families of Sunday revelers who had the right of way. Or so they thought, and so did the white-gloved gendarme who was directing matters from the center of the intersection. He whistled me down. I stopped on the arc of the turn and watched through the rear-view while he descended on me in slow imperious strides. Behind him the traffic was already starting to snarl, and it was going to take him the rest of the morning to untangle it. But he didn't seem to care.

Before he got to me, I had my head out the window.

"Look, Officer," I said in my best Yakima American,

"I'm sorry as hell but I've got a plane to catch. Is this the right way to the airport?"

It's a dumb enough tactic, but I've never known it to fail. He touched his fingers to his kepi. I could see the hesitation writ large in his eyes.

"It may sound crazy," I went on, "but my mother's just had twins! Can you imagine that? *Twins?* At her age? I just got the telegram this morning. You just can't keep the old girl down! But the thing is, I don't know whether I've got two new brothers or two new sisters or one of each, and the telegram didn't say. Can you imagine? So I've got to go home to find out, only home is in Yakima, that's in the state of Washington, and that means I've got to catch the wagon train out of Seattle which leaves every Monday morning at . . ."

Somewhere in there he asked me for my papers, but I gave him no mercy. I was making like an airplane. I had my head down out the window and my arms swept back inside the Giulia and behind him the horns were blowing like it was Bastille Day and New Year's Eve rolled into one.

"Airport!" I shouted at him in the din. "AIR! PORT!"

Dumb enough, like I say, but pretty near foolproof, and if you work on your French, you can probably get away with it on the San Diego Freeway.

Finally he shouted back, "*Fous-moi la paix!*" which, broadly translated, means "Fuck off!" He pointed down the N16 and white-gloved me on. I didn't give him time to change his mind.

The Renault van, though, was nowhere in sight. I was beginning to feel like one of J.-C. Fleurie's minions. I pulled into the first gas station I came to, unfolded my map, and then saw right away what had happened. Because if the quickest way to Chantilly was the autoroute, the shortest was this very same Nationale 16. In other words, L'Isle-Adam had been scratched, and unless Bernard Lascault had yet another hideaway in the northern suburbs, they were headed right for Cookie's.

I set the Giulia on the automatic pilot and stuck her in high. Some twenty kilometers up the road, in a place called Luzarches, I caught up with them. I had a crazy passing notion that if I'd wanted to, I could have taken them right there, on the highway, made off with the two Rillington-Blumenstocks, gone back to Paris and copped the real one, and set up shop for myself. B. F. Cage, *courtier en tableaux.* But it was only passing—the product, maybe, of too much Al Dove—and more to the point was the idea that the reception committee still waiting for me in Lascault's apartment might be only part of the overall muscle. Because unless I missed my guess, Bernard Lascault had flown home from L.A. on a group plan.

Instead, then, I gave the van plenty of room, and when they entered the little village and turned to squeeze down the alley, I kept on going to the next town. Because suddenly there was no hurry at all. None at all. I had time for a basket of croissants in the local café and a double *express*, and even a telephone chat with my friend Dedini.

Monsieur le Commissaire was in his usual foul mood, heightened by his having been up half the night. And on a wild goose chase, and one set off by yours truly. No, they hadn't found Al Dove in the métro. All they'd found was damaged government property. Dedini wanted Al Dove and Binty Dove and me, all at once. That was nothing new, but now he added Helen Raven and William Rillington to his list.

I told Dedini to sit tight. I was working on something, a plan, I'd call him later on. If he wanted to keep busy in the meantime, there were three stiffs over in Lascault's apartment who needed a fourth for bridge. Only he shouldn't knock before entering.

I hung up, paid for breakfast and the call, and went back outside to the Giulia. I started missing Dedini almost immediately. I also missed the Giulia, once I'd parked her again and gotten out. This was just outside the village, almost exactly at the place where I'd turned around on my first visit. I missed Pierrot the Nosepicker, too. At times like that a man needs all the friends he can get, but the only candidates I spotted when I skirted through the fields were a couple of peasants who looked like they belonged in somebody's landscape, and they paid me no attention once they saw I wasn't carrying an easel.

The wall was of stone and uniformly higher than my head. I chose a likely spot and pulled myself up. No siren went off, at least that I could hear, and a thick copse of poplars screened me from humanity. But suddenly, as I dropped down on the inside, I realized that I'd no plan at all.

FIFTEEN

THE BREAKFAST ROOM WAS a cozy fishbowl affair, somewhat smaller than an exhibition hall, that bubbled out behind the mansion into some tulip beds. The Lascaults were receiving there that beautiful Sunday, Monsieur in white ducks and an elegant white turtleneck, Madame in a two-piece white ensemble of some light jersey material. The staff also wore white. In fact the only people who didn't were the guests. Of these there were three, two of them invited. The invited ones were a pair of art-loving Californians called Binty Dove and Johnny Vee, sometimes known as "the Alligator." The uninvited one was also from the shores of the Pacific, but not much of an art lover.

They were already into the scrambled eggs and kippers when I arrived. I took another coffee, just to be sociable. The field hand who'd brought me there seemed to want to hang around to make sure I drank it, but the only white on him was in his eyeballs and when Johnny Vee told him to beat it, he beat it. We'd only just met. This was outside one of the outbuildings I'd spotted coming through the trees and which was where, to judge from the Renault van parked next to it, the master and mistress kept the overflow of their collection. A considerable sweep of lawn separated it from the main house, and I was standing in its shadow, deciding my next move, when he made up my mind for me. "Lift 'em, ofay," he said behind me. I lifted my arms and the rest of my body lifted with them, helped out by the forearm under my chin. He shook me down, and then he kept a respectful few paces in back of me while we crossed the sward.

The sun had turned the windows of the house into one-way mirrors. This gave them plenty of time to get their signals straight. Still there was one of those awkward silences when I came in, understandable enough, though, when you remember that around about then I was supposed to be all stretched out in Bernard Lascault's apartment with my arms folded across my chest and a rose between my teeth.

Finally my hostess invited me to sit down. Johnny Vee seconded the motion.

"Siddown, Cage," he said.

Freddy Schwartz had mentioned him. I only knew him slightly, and I'd never had any wish to deepen the relationship. I knew that his real name was more complicated than Johnny Vee, also that he'd picked up his nickname on the L.A. high-school basketball courts. Later on he'd played college ball in California and he'd been good too. Some claimed he'd thrown away a career in the pros Maybe so, but still in his early thirties, he was already called the heir apparent, and his daddy, they said, owned a whole pro league among his so-called legitimate enterprises.

In Chantilly, France, though, the Alligator was a long way from home. I think he felt it too, and reacted by trying to throw his weight around.

I didn't sit down right away, though that had less to do with him than with what I saw over their heads. They weren't hung, only propped up on chairs. Two chairs to each, and they took up most of the wall space in the room that wasn't glass. There were people in these paintings too, but they weren't portraits, more like studies of architecture and space, formal and weird at the same time, with balconies and archways and windows opening onto scenes that seemed to belong to some totally other time and place. I don't know what you'd call them, and whether they were worth all the fuss is another question, but like the portrait they too seemed painted within an inch of their lives, and to my unpracticed eye they sure looked like they came from the same brush.

"What do you think of them, Mr. Cage?" asked my hostess.

I sat down then, between her and Johnny Vee, with Binty and Bernard Lascault across from me.

"More to the point," I said, "is what *you* think of them, Mrs. Lascault. Do they measure up to your expectations?"

She gazed at me blandly—a sociable, aristocratic expression.

"They certainly do," she said. "Of course it's only a first impression—you realize this is the first time I've

seen them—but I think they're beautiful, marvelous.
I'm very surprised, I must admit."

"Then you're going to buy them?"

"*Buy* them?" She seemed to enjoy the idea. "No, I
should think not."

"How come? Is the price too high?"

"Not at all. The truth is: I haven't had to pay anything for them. Not one sou. You see, they're a gift."

"A gift? Who from?"

"Why, from all these people," she said, gesturing
magnanimously. "But most particularly," turning to
him, "from my dear husband."

I couldn't make out the slightest irony in her voice.
The joke, it seemed, if there was one, was on me.

I stared across at Binty and Lascault.

"I'm glad to hear at least that you haven't paid for
them," I said, fixing them. "The way I understand it,
they may be fakes."

I like to think I saw the nerves jump in Binty's
cheeks. At least that. But Bernard Lascault didn't so
much as swallow. I wondered if, like Al Dove, they'd
known all along. Or only suspected.

"Fakes?" Cookie Lascault echoed to my left.

"That's right. Painted by a man called William Rillington."

"Well then," she went on without a quaver, "hats off
to the painter!"

It was my turn to be surprised. She'd straightened
out of her habitual drooping posture, but without any
of the stiffness of the dame in the portrait or the shrew
I'd seen in action. Her gaze now had scorn in it min-

gled with commiseration, the look of someone who's
got the upper hand and knows it.

"I wonder how well acquainted you are with the
history of Art, Mr. Cage. Not a great deal, I'd suppose.
Otherwise you would know that history is full of works
that have been re-identified and re-attributed at one
time or another: the Cranachs, the Watteaus, the
whole *school* of Rubens, for example. But does that
lower their value in any way? Do the museums take
them off their walls? A great painting is a great painting, Mr. Cage, no matter who painted it."

The lesson, I thought momentarily, was over, but
she was only warming to her subject.

"You called these fakes, Mr. Cage. But what does
that mean? Fakes of what, after all? They're not *copies*,
are they? Of course not. John . . . John Blumenstock
could never have painted them. Not if he'd lived a
hundred years. But your artist . . . what was his
name . . . ?"

She snapped her fingers, searching for it.

"Rillington," I supplied.

"Rillington. *Rillington* painted them, Mr. Cage.
With his own two hands, starting from raw canvas. At
the most he worked in the style of, *à la manière de.* But
since when is it wrong or bad for one artist to be
inspired by another? Where is the fakery in that?"

The shrill had come back, but different from the
one I knew, full of gaiety and triumph. I didn't get it in
so many words, but the reason for it may have had
nothing to do with art history. She'd said it herself:
John Blumenstock could never have painted them. In her

weird cracked way, maybe she was getting even at last.

Besides, they hadn't cost her a centime.

"Where is the fakery, Mr. Cage?" she repeated loudly.

"Well," I said, "there's the little question of attribution. I'd say . . ."

"Attribution?" she interrupted. "Ah yes. Who painted them. I see what you mean. But that's only money, Mr. Cage, crass money. The market. Right now a Blumenstock may be worth a fortune, while your Rillington is unknown. But who is to say that a hundred years from now, when posterity judges, the positions won't be reversed? In any event, all that has nothing to do with the paintings or their real value. It's paltry, ephemeral, of no importance. The sickness of our times, if you will. People make a great commotion over nothing. Art is eternal, Mr. Cage. But the people who make the commotion, the promoters, the dealers . . . ," this with a nod at the company present, "even the collectors . . . ," with a self-mocking laugh. "We're nothing but fools, Mr. Cage. Here today and gone tomorrow. A pack of fools."

She seemed to have finished. I glanced at the others. They had nothing to add. On the contrary, they were perfectly happy to let her say it for them. I looked at the paintings, then out past Johnny Vee at the sunswept grounds, and the message came across loud and clear: all was well in Chantilly and the world, and the only one out of step was yours truly.

"I'm glad to hear you taking such a lofty, long-range view, Mrs. Lascault," I said. "The only trouble is that in all the commotion that's been going on over these pictures, a lot of people have been getting pushed around. I happen to be one of them, but that's the least of it. Two of them are dead, and a third would be but for a matter of a couple of centimeters. Maybe that's of no importance either, but . . ."

"I wouldn't know anything about that," she interrupted coldly.

"No?" I said. "Well, maybe you wouldn't at that, the world has a way of protecting you rich folks. But I'd venture to say your husband here does, even though he mightn't admit it. And Mrs. Dove too. Not to say the celebrated art dealer on my right."

I could feel the vibrations of hostility coming from him. I paid them no attention.

"There's also the question of the police, paltry and of no importance as they may be, but they're also making a commotion and this time they may not be so ready to stop. What's more, if I'm not mistaken the shooting's not yet over. Far from it. I can't figure out what else our friend the Alligator's doing this far from home. I mean, Vegas is a lot more his style than Chantilly, and I don't imagine he came all this way just to peddle some pictures. Tell me, Johnny boy," I said, turning to him finally, "who's on your hit list besides me? Al Dove? Helen Raven? What about Binty here, maybe she's on it too?"

He was halfway out of his chair, and his face had gone white. Maybe mine had too.

"You're all washed up, Cage," he snarled.

I couldn't help laughing at him.

"Fuck it, Johnny," I said. "Why in hell do you guys always have to come on like a bad Cagney movie?"

"Shut up!" Cookie Lascault shrilled behind me. "Both of you!"

He did, but I turned on her.

"No, maybe you don't know about all that," I said, "but your husband sure as hell does, and either way it doesn't add much luster to your reputation." I pointed at him across the table. "What was it you said, Mr. Lascault? That Paris isn't Chicago? But if that's true, all you've got to do is bring Chicago in, right? It's as old as the movies: the hitmen from out of town. You buy off your wife with a couple of worthless paintings, you buy off the police too, and then you bring in your imported muscle to take care of anybody who squawks. It's a costly affair maybe, and you've blown your Blumenstock racket in the bargain, but at the same time you've eliminated the middle man, right? Now it's just you and your silent partner here. Tell me, Johnny boy," I said, turning back to him, "what's your percentage of next year's take?"

This time the Alligator only laughed at me from his chair. But Binty and Bernard Lascault didn't so much as crack a smile, and as for Cookie, I realized that I'd misread her pretty badly. Whatever she knew, it was pretty clear she didn't give a damn.

As long as she got hers.

It was very quiet in the room. I felt like I'd been throwing punches in a plastic bag. A regular old windmill. I had one left, call it the Yakima Haymaker, and though I didn't suppose it would bring the fans cheering to their feet, I threw it anyway, just for the hell of it.

"One other thing, Mrs. Lascault," I said. "There's

the question of the portrait. The so-called fake Blumenstock, which turns out to be the only genuine one. It's only a Blumenstock though, and from what you've just said about posterity, I take it you're no longer interested?"

"On the contrary," she replied, drooping again and fixing me with that cool aristocratic stare. "It's a lovely painting in my opinion. I'm still very much interested."

"And your offer still holds?"

"My offer?"

"The last time we met, you mentioned a certain figure."

I detected a flicker of interest on Bernard Lascault's part.

"Yes, I did," she replied. "But circumstances have changed. In addition, that offer was for three paintings. Now there is only one."

"That doesn't sound very fair to William Rillington."

"*Fair?*" She snorted, tossing her head. "But artists have never had decent compensation for their work! Although, under different circumstances, I would be happy to talk to Mr. Rillington about his future."

What is it about the rich? I began in my mind. But she broke in on the refrain, saying:

"As far as the portrait is concerned, I would consider twelve thousand dollars more than adequate now."

Twelve thousand dollars. A little more than fifty thousand francs, but not much more. It was the old auction price. Al Dove had huffed and puffed, but now the air was coming out of the balloon and Cookie Lascault was exacting her last revenge.

"I know where it is, Mrs. Lascault," I said. "I can get it for you."

I made a mistake before. I said I never saw her smile again. But there it came, right then, folding her skin into hard and gleaming creases.

Bernard Lascault started to answer for her, but she waved him off.

"That won't be necessary," she answered. "In fact I'm afraid I've no longer any need of your services, Mr. Cage. You see, the . . . the present owner has been in touch with me herself. We are already in the process of negotiating the sale."

The Yakima Haymaker had missed. I was flat on my ass, and the referee was counting. I had no particular wish to get up either, and the spectators were already heading for the exits. Binty Dove, the love of my life, had her eyes averted, maybe she couldn't stand the sight of blood, and Johnny Vee, the fight promoter, was motioning to some of his muscle to come scrape the loser off the canvas.

They broke out of the landscape and came for me. One was black and the other white, which only goes to show how public-spirited the mob's gotten, but otherwise there wasn't much to choose between them. They were big and dumb-looking, and even in my better days I wouldn't have wanted to take either of them on without an elephant gun.

They led me back across the lawn to one of the outbuildings and stuck me inside with the dead wood. There weren't any windows in this one and little furniture, only a miscellany of gardening equipment and enough cut timber to keep the Lascaults warm for the next decade or so, if ever the Allah-worshippers started tinkering with the oil spigots again. The rich, I guess, think of everything.

I pulled up a log and sat down, and it was there that I had the first of several distinctly unmemorable conversations with the Alligator.

SIXTEEN

CHANCES ARE he has his qualities, and I'm sure he loves his mother. But he was a lousy judge of human psychology—mine to begin with—and he couldn't resist shooting his mouth off.

He started in on Al Dove. Dove, he called him. Dove had him choked up to the windpipe, he wanted Dove in the worst way. Dove, he said, had crossed the Organization for the last time. The Organization had decided to write him off.

"Where is he, Cage?" said Johnny Vee.

"I don't know."

He chuckled, a hard rattley sound.

"At least that's an improvement on your subway story," he said.

"What subway story?"

"The one you told the French Law. That he was locked in the Paris subway. Maybe you can get away with that cockamamie bullshit on the French Law. I want the truth."

There, if you see what I mean. A small disclosure maybe, but the only people I'd told about the métro were Police Judiciaire. The Police Judiciaire at least knew that it wasn't cockamamie bullshit. But maybe what the Police Judiciaire knew and what they were letting on these days to their brothers in the other branches were two different things.

"What are you going to do to get it, Johnny boy?" I said. "Rearrange my knuckles for me?"

He looked at me a minute. Then the look turned into a sneer.

"What is it that makes punks like you stick together?" he asked.

He turned to the muscle.

"D'you know what Dove did to this punk?" he asked them.

The muscle shook their heads from side to side, and back.

"This punk used all his suck with the Law to help Dove beat a rap. Dove was peddling dope in West-wood—can you imagine that?—and the Law nailed him. And this punk stepped in and made a deal for him, even though it meant embarrassing some people who didn't want to be embarrassed. And d'you know how Dove paid him back?"

He waited for the muscle to shake their heads again.

They did.

"*Dove stole his snatch!*"

Johnny Vee thought this punchline very funny. He

gave it the big alligator laugh. So did the muscle. Then Johnny Vee stopped laughing, and so did the muscle.

"So how come, Cage? How come punks like you always stick together?"

"It seems to me you ought to know better than me," I said.

"What does that mean?"

"Well, maybe he took me once, if you want to look at it like that, but how many times has the mob . . . excuse me, the Organization . . . gone to the wall with him? Let me see, there was dope all right, and then the Rancho del Cielo deal—that was a beaut, wasn't it?—and now there's Art. Either somebody upstairs must be pretty dumb, else the . . . Organization is having a hell of a time recruiting competent personnel. Present company excepted, of course."

He started to answer back, something about how he was changing that, but then he stopped in midstream.

"Let's cut the bullshit, Cage," he said. "Where is he?"

"Like I told you, Johnny boy," I answered, "I don't have the foggiest."

I thought he was going to slug me. He didn't though. He turned on his heels and went out, and one of the muscle took up guard duty outside the door and the other inside, facing me, though after a while they changed places, to make it more interesting.

All in all, it wasn't much of a performance. I mean, if you're going to try to scare information out of some one, you've got to follow through. Instead Johnny Vee left me to my thoughts, and the more I thought, the more it occurred to me that something must have gone wrong, that they had some other use for me—a notion that got all the stronger the longer I waited. So that when they finally got around to the rough stuff, I was pretty sure they were only funning.

Though I didn't know it at the time, I had help too . . . from the least likely source.

Because all that morning the phone kept ringing in the main house. Each time it rang, the technicians went to work, trying to trace it. And they did too, apparently. Only once she was calling from the Champs Élysées, another time from a café over by the Odéon, another time from the Gare du Nord. The Professor was really jumping around town that morning, without rhyme or reason, and every time she dialed Chantilly, she changed the rules of the game. Maybe somewhere buried in the archives of the Service de la Répression des Fraudes Artistiques you could still find the tapes of those conversations, though I'd be inclined to doubt it, but they must have been something to hear. Because if Cookie Lascault thought at one point that she was going to be able to have her cake for twelve thousand bucks, she was dead wrong. The certainty must have changed into hope, and then the hope too went up in an explosion of vengeance and vilification. Along the way the price kept shifting too, and so did the method of payment. At the next-to-the-last call, Cookie was to come herself, alone, with cash in a suitcase. Apparently she agreed to that too, at least over the phone. But Helen Raven had the last word, and if I wasn't there to listen in, I can still imagine the gist of it: *Suppose I decide not to sell it at any price! Suppose that's my price: no price!*

I learned some of this from Johnny Vee. I couldn't say exactly at what stage in the negotiations he came back into the woodshed, only that they must have taken a sour turn by then. If Cookie Lascault hadn't panicked yet, she was at least willing to let him try it his way. Not that he sullied his own hands. We had a brief question-and-answer period, not a very satisfactory one from his point of view, and then he simply loosed the muscle on me. There wasn't much I could do about it. I covered up while I could, and took it, the kind of classic impersonal battering the mob teaches its boys in kindergarten.

They propped me up on a stool when they were done and held me there. I was swallowing a mixture of blood and saliva, but when my tongue worked its way around my teeth, they were all present and accounted for. Funning, like I said. Johnny Vee leaned over me and asked me again where the picture was. I looked up at him, grinning through the tears, and told him to go fuck himself. He gave me a shot himself then, for the folks back home, but I hardly felt a thing, and when he turned and went out again, I knew in some weird way that things were looking up.

The second wait was shorter than the first. Through the open door I saw him standing in the sunlight, some halfway across the lawn. He shouted something to the muscle outside the door and motioned with his arm. They delivered me to him.

The sun felt good. A light breeze dried my sweat,

and walking took some of the wobble out of my legs. Johnny Vee led me inside, into a deep-pile bathroom with scented soap, gold-leafed spigots and towels as soft as cashmere. I looked at my face in the mirror. One of the eyes was almost closed. I did what I could about the rest of it, even making a few passes with an electric razor provided for guests, and though the result mightn't have won any beauty contests, well, I'd seen worse.

"Let's go, Cage," said Johnny Vee.

He was standing near the door, his arms folded across his chest. I went up to him. Under the circumstances it couldn't have been much more than a love tap, but I let him have it anyway, high on his alligator snout. Just for fun.

He took it like a man.

Breakfast was long since over. The company had moved into the drawing room, the one with all the paintings I'd seen on my first visit, and Cookie Lascault was slumped in that same high-backed white chair that molded around her body.

Things may have been looking up, but you'd never have known it from her. Well, you could say, a dame her age isn't likely to get any better as the day goes on, but to look at her then you'd have to wonder if she was going to make it till tea-time. Her hair had gone scraggly, her eyes dull, and her skin had that shiny pallor to it that made you think inevitably of Hammond organs and Forest Lawn. Maybe Johnny Vee's boys had worked me over pretty good, but they had

nothing on whoever'd done it to her—a realization, I
confess, that perked me up considerably.

"I want to talk to Mr. Cage," she said when I came in.
"Alone."

There was some objection to this.

"Out," she ordered. "All of you. I want to talk to him
alone."

She waved in the direction of the doors. They
started to file out. Then she changed her mind.

"You stay," she said, pointing at her husband. "I may
need you."

Bernard Lascault stayed. When the others had left
he sat down. So did I.

"I've had a harrowing morning, Mr. Cage," said
Cookie Lascault. "There's been enough shilly-shally. I
want that painting. I want it now."

It hurt too much to raise an eyebrow, but I couldn't
resist a few choice remarks. About the sale she'd been
supposed to be negotiating, for one thing, and the
Alligator for another.

She dismissed them with a deprecating gesture.

"You already know what I think of . . . of Helen
Raven," she said. "The events of this morning have
only confirmed my opinion. I needn't go into it
further. As for what they've done to you, I'm not sorry.
You probably had it coming to you. You'll live. But I
want that painting. Now. You said you know where it
is. I assume you can go get it."

Just like that, with one snap of the fingers.

I thought about it briefly.

"Yes, I might be able to," I answered.

"Then do it," she said. "I have no conditions."

I grinned at her, feeling my skin crack, but she hadn't meant it as a joke.

"Well I might have a few," I said.

"Name them. Be quick about it."

"Money, first of all."

"How much?"

"Well, the last time we met, you were talking about half a million francs."

"That was for three paintings."

"I know. And circumstances keep changing, don't they? I'd say half would be fair. Say, two hundred and fifty thou . . ."

"Go get my checkbook," she interrupted. Even though she didn't call him by name, he knew who she was talking to.

But I shook my head.

"Cash," I said. "No offense intended, but I'll take it in cash."

For the first time that day, I saw some expression in Bernard Lascault's face. Call it consternation.

"Two hundred and fifty thousand francs!" he objected. "We don't have that much in the . . ."

"Go get it," she interrupted imperiously. "As much as we have. Bring it to me."

He was gone quite a while. I like to think he had to slit open their conjugal mattress. But when he came back, it was with one of those old-fashioned brown leather briefcases, and the briefcase was stuffed to the gunwales with printed legal tender, courtesy of the Banque de France.

He put it on the coffee table between us.

"How much is in there?" she asked him.

"A little over 160,000," he said.

"Is that all we have?"

"That's all, at least until . . ."

"We'll call it 160,000. You'll have to take the rest in a check, Mr. Cage. Ninety thousand francs. Once you've delivered the painting."

Haggling to the end. I would have grinned at her in appreciation, but it hurt me to grin. Besides, I had other conditions to fulfill.

The first was purely technical. I had no intention of coming back to Chantilly if I could help it, and I wanted the Giulia delivered to my hotel. I tossed Bernard Lascault the keys. To my surprise, he caught them.

Then there was the little matter of my letter from the Prefecture of Police.

"You may not know anything about this either, Mrs. Lascault, but I'm walking around with a twenty-four-hour expulsion notice in my pocket. It runs out at midnight tonight. I want that lifted."

"It will be," she said.

"Who'll take care of that? You or Bernard?"

"I will," her husband put in.

"Once the painting's been delivered, of course," she said. "Is that all?"

"Not quite. I don't want any of Johnny Vee's boys coming along for the ride. Or your friends from the police either. When I get the painting I'll let you know where to pick it up, but in between I want a free hand. Is that clear?"

They both nodded.

"Then there's just one other thing," I said. "I want one of you to go along with me. To protect your interests, if you want to look at it that way."

Bernard Lascault started to protest. I guess he thought I meant him.

"Who?" said Cookie Lascault, cutting him off.

"Mrs. Dove," I answered.

SEVENTEEN

AT THAT YOU HAVE TO GIVE them credit. I'm talking
about the so-called oppressed sex. The next time one
of them starts laying the sob story on you, complete
with equal job opportunities, you tell her about Cookie
Lascault.

And Binty Dove.

Once we'd left the village, I stopped the van. Then
she pushed her shades up onto her head and threw her
arms around me. I winced, and she drew back, and
tears welled in her eyes, big real ones, and the tips of
her fingers grazed my wounds.

"My God," she said. "What did they do to you, you
poor baby?"

"Oh, they were only fooling around,' I said. "They
just got a little carried away."

"I couldn't stand it," she said. "When they took you
away, I couldn't stand it. But what was I to do?"

"Yeah," I said. "It was like that this morning too. At Bernard's apartment."

"You mean you were *there*?"

"That's right. I was out in the street. I guess it was a lucky thing I showed up early, honh?"

"Oh Cagey, I was so scared."

"Sure," I said. "I could tell that from down the block. I was dying to tell you everything was all right. Only there didn't seem any way, under the circumstances."

"But what was I to do, Cagey? Ever since they got here last night, Johnny and the others. I was so scared. I wanted to warn you, but how could I? They never let me out of their sight."

"And yesterday afternoon, before they got here? You were scared then too, weren't you?"

"Of course I was. I had no idea who was following us. Then when you went off like that . . . and he came after me . . ."

"And you couldn't go back to the apartment, could you?" I finished for her. "Obviously. Because that's where the paintings were. So you took him out to L'Isle-Adam where you knew you could lay a trap on him. Or get help. Right?"

She didn't answer.

Like I say, there's a form of honesty in silence.

Then I asked her—just for the record, because God knows it didn't matter anymore—when she'd gotten to Paris. She didn't answer that either.

"But that night after Al's party?" I said. "In the studio? You were there then, weren't you, Binty?"

Her chin dropped, and the wet cheeks.

"Yes I was, Cagey. I was there."

We drove off then. She asked me if I was sure I could drive. I said I'd always wanted to see how the Renault van handled. It did all right too, in a trucky sort of way. But she wasn't finished talking, not by a long shot. The important thing was: we were free. We were free, weren't we? Free at last, with all those awful things behind us? She didn't know how I'd swung it, how I'd convinced them to let us go, and she didn't care. The important thing was that it was done, behind us, and all we had to do was forget it. And we would forget it, wouldn't we? Yes we would. She would see to that.

But of course she cared. Just a little. She'd seen the briefcase too, and she either knew or guessed what was in it.

"How'd you do it, darling?" she asked. This was on the autoroute. "How'd you talk them into letting us go?"

"Oh," I said, "I can be a pretty persuasive fellow when I want to be."

"But where are we going? Where are we going now?"

"Well, first we've got some property of yours to collect. Remember?"

"You mean the painting? My God, can't we just forget about it? Why don't we just go around Paris and keep on going? What's to stop us? They'll never find us. Eventually they'll give up trying. We can send them a postcard telling them where it is. That's all they care about."

"What about the Law?"

"Well what about it? There's nothing they can prove."

Maybe so and maybe not. Though I was inclined to give her the nod.

"Well where do you want to go, Binty?" I asked.

"Somewhere where there are palms and soft breezes?"

She didn't get the reference. There was no reason she should.

"Why not?" she answered. "Why the hell not? Or some place where it's freezing cold and there's ice on the pine cones! Hot or cold, what difference does it make? Don't you understand? All I want to do is be with you, you dummy, don't you understand that?"

And I did, in a way. That was the funny part. Back at the Lascaults' breakfast I'd tried something on for size, about Johnny Vee's hit list, and the more I thought about it the more obvious it seemed to me. Because once the Blumenstock affair was over, where was the need for the middle man? Or woman? In other words, once Arts Mondiaux had opened direct contact with their suppliers, hadn't both Doves become expendable? It stood to reason, and whatever Bernard or Johnny Vee had in mind for her, the idea must have occurred to Binty too.

When I pulled into the service station on the auto-route she all but threw a fit. We didn't need gas, she said, what was I stopping for? Not for gas, I said. I had to make a phone call. But I wasn't going to leave her alone in the van, was I? Sure I was, I said, but I'd be in the phone booth right alongside. Still she grabbed my hand when I started to get out, grabbed it hard, and while I was calling and she could easily have jumped into the driver's seat . . . no, she just sat there, frozen, her small face staring out at me through the passenger's window.

Of course it didn't help that I took the keys and the briefcase into the booth with me.

Maybe by then she'd spotted our company too. Parked back on the Chantilly byroad, I'd been a little surprised by the traffic, even for a pretty Sunday, but I'd been as willing as not to chalk it up to chance and paranoia. But there was no mistaking them in the service area. They came in a black unmarked Renault 16, but with an antenna big enough to receive Gibraltar. They drove through between the gas pumps without stopping and parked far down, near the access road, and waited while I told Dedini about them.

The rich, it seemed, keep their word just like the rest of us.

I told Dedini I was ready to deliver three of the people he wanted, but that it had to be done my way, and that I needed his help. I explained what I had in mind. It took some time. At first he didn't like it at all. Then he gave me some static because of the logistics involved, followed by a long pause while he put it together from his end. I told him where I was, and he estimated how long he'd need and when I should leave the service station, and all the while Binty Dove stared out through the two windows that separated us, with the shades up in her hair.

"Who was that you were talking to?" she wanted to know when I came out. "Was it Al?"

"No, it wasn't Al."

"But you're going to kill me, aren't you, Cagey? The two of you?"

She had killing on the brain all right. I guess after a while it gets to be pretty commonplace.

"No," I said, opening the door on her side. "At least not right now. Right now I'm going to buy you a cup of coffee."

We went inside into the restaurant section. It was one of those typical autoroute joints, indistinguishable from one country to the next except that the ones in France are more expensive and the food worse. I had a cheese omelette to go with the coffee, but Binty seemed to have lost her appetite. The thing was, she said, she was so exhausted, done in, she didn't care what happened to her so long as I stayed with her. She felt like it had been years since she'd had a real night's sleep. She felt like a long time back somebody had put her on a treadmill, like a laboratory mouse, and she'd been running ever since, around and around and around, chasing her tail without ever catching it.

I paid the check and we went back to the Renault van. I put her in the passenger's seat and closed the door, then walked around to my side and got in. The grass was an unnatural green under the sun, and not a blade was stirring.

"Wait a minute, Cagey," she said, putting her hand on mine as I turned the key in the slot. Her eyes were big with message. "Just think a minute before we go. Make sure you know what you want."

She gripped my hand for emphasis.

I thought about it a minute. I'm sorry, baby, I thought, but you've fed me to the wolves once too often. Then I turned the key again, and threw the van into reverse, and then into first.

They'd set up the first roadblock just where the autoroute ended, at the Porte de la Chapelle. It was a hell of a place to do it, and on a Sunday in addition, and if it had been a couple of hours later, they'd have created a jam all the way back to the Belgian border. As it was, and even though they didn't have to check every car, the lines were already half a kilometer long by the time we got there. I'd been trying to spot our company, without luck. The Renault 16 had stayed in the service area, but I was pretty sure somebody else would have taken over, ahead of us or behind.

I'd given Dedini a description of the van. When we got to the head of our file, the gendarme in charge waved us through without a second glance. Then we were into Paris, and I zigged and zagged the van through some side streets before coming out around Stalingrad and the top of the Canal St. Martin.

But at least one car had been ahead of us, waiting. It was another Renault 16, and I didn't pick him up till we were part way down the canal. When I stopped suddenly for a red light, though, he had no choice but to snuggle up behind me, and I could clearly see the turtle's head trying to hide in the passenger's seat. It belonged to none other than my old friend, Commissaire Ravier.

I couldn't have run them if I'd wanted to, not in that van. As it was, I didn't want to. But it was a good thing I'd taken out some insurance of my own.

The second roadblock was already in place on the

east side of the canal. The Law, Dedini's Law, had cordoned off an area several blocks deep, starting in from the quays, and they were there in force, in plainclothes and uniform, and the only other people in sight were some fishermen sunning themselves on the canal bank.

There was a checkpoint on the far end of the bridge, another on the Quai de Jemmapes itself. We passed both without a challenge, but the Renault 16 got stopped behind us. I saw Ravier get out, gesticulating like a proper Frenchman. But another proper Frenchman was there to match him, a big and gray-jawed one, and it's a shame I can't quote you their conversation.

We turned onto the side street. Like Dedini had promised, there wasn't a cop in sight, just the low-scarred façades of the warehouses. I parked and got out, Lascault's briefcase in hand. Binty got out on the other side.

The skylight glinted brightly in the sun.

"You mean it's been there all this time?" Binty said, gazing up at the building.

"No, not all this time."

"Jesus."

"They ran out of places to hide. It's too bad you didn't think of it."

"Who's up there now. Is Al up there?"

"I doubt it."

"Or the police?"

"I don't know. We'll see."

This seemed to reassure her momentarily. But half-way up the dim stairs, with the garbage smell full in our nostrils, she pulled hard on my hand again. I thought it was to steady herself. Maybe it was. But then the plea came, hoarsely this time even though she was talking in a whisper:

"God, Cagey, please get me out of this."

I knocked on the door at the top landing.

"Come in," Helen Raven called from inside. "The door is open."

We went in. She was alone, staring down into the street from the skylight. Al Dove had said something about needing an army, but the door was open and all Helen Raven had for her defense was a gun. It looked like the same one she'd carried the night before. It hung listlessly in her hand, as though she'd forgotten it was there.

The studio had undergone an extraordinary transformation. A week or so before, it had struck me as unlived in. Now it reminded me of one of those hermit's apartments you read about from time to time, when the neighbors complain of the smell and the police break in to find the bodies molding and the old newspapers stacked to the ceilings. Not that there was so much stuff, but you got the feeling every dish in the place had been used more than once, with no washing in between, and the smell was stale and heavy with turpentine. The floor was awash in papers, oily rags, clothes, cigarette butts, with the biggest piles around the easels, and though the sun was streaming in through the skylight, the spots shone down on the portrait of John Blumenstock and his wife.

"Find a seat," said Helen Raven, scarcely looking at us. "She hasn't come yet."

"Who are you waiting for, Professor?" I asked her.
"Who am I waiting for," she repeated in a mono-
tone. "I'm waiting for Judith."

"Judith?" I said. But she didn't seem to hear, and
then it struck me who Judith was, though probably
nobody had called her that since her nanny.

I put the briefcase down. I asked her where Rillington was. She didn't seem to know, or care particularly.
She said he'd gone out a while ago, but in a way that
suggested it might have been a quarter of an hour or a
week, or anything in between. As it happened, it was
closer to a quarter of an hour, and the Law, not taking
any chances, had picked him up. But that had been out
of her line of vision, in more ways than one. All that she
saw, all that she was capable of seeing, was the street
immediately below and, I suppose, the limousine that
was supposed to pull up there any minute.

"She's not coming, Helen," I said finally. "Cookie's
not coming. Judith. She's sent us instead."

The message didn't seem to register.

"But she's buying the painting," I added. "I've
brought as much cash as she had. There's a little over
160,000 francs in the bag here, with more to come on
delivery."

Again no response. But a moment later she turned
from the skylight and came toward us. I felt Binty
stiffen beside me. I did too, though less from the gun
than from the expression on her face. Or rather: the
lack of expression. The mouth was slack, the skin
pocked and dotted with bumps, the eyes small and
bored and unseeing. It was the moon woman in short,

the walking zombie, and you'd never in a million years have guessed the violence seething below the crust.

As it was, she dropped the gun on the work table near the easels. She rummaged in the mess for a cigarette, found a pack but it was empty, crumpled it, tossed it on the floor. Then she found another, turned and asked us for a light. I produced a box of matches. She took them from me and lit up with a steady hand, contributing Gauloise smoke to the general turpentine stink, and stood next to us, her arms now folded across her chest, studying the painting.

"It's a great one," she said finally, in that same toneless voice. "The best he ever did."

She went on talking then. About the painting, about him, about them. Them was John Blumenstock and his wife. In its way, Helen Raven's version of Cookie was one of the most violent diatribes I'd ever heard, but the horror of it came less from the words than the tone, and not from the female hysterics you'd expect but from the utter absence of same. It was a little short on coherence, but the gist was clear enough: simply that the artist she, Helen Raven, had taken over from the woman on the canvas was already a human ruin, a wreck, a shambles at thirty-four. And this thanks to the woman on the canvas. Having seen the original in action, I'd have to add that the Professor's portrait came closer to reality than the painter's, but it came out flat and colorless, and with all the awful finality of an obituary.

Maybe it takes one woman to do real justice to another.

The briefcase with the money was almost directly under her feet. She bent down, opened it, rummaged idly inside. She stood back up, clutching a random fistful of bills. The suggestion of a smile tightened her lips.

"I told you," she said, staring at the portrait. "Won't anybody believe me? It's not for sale. It's simply not for sale."

"I can see your point of view, Helen," I answered, "but a lot of people have gone to a lot of trouble over this painting. The money's not all for you either. Half of it's Al's."

"Al's?" she asked distantly.

She started to laugh, a far-off sound that seemed to come from somewhere outside her.

"But Al's dead," she said. "I killed him."

She gazed around vaguely, as if remembering the murder weapon, then swiveled sharply. Too sharply almost. She caught herself, then focused on Binty.

"But you're his wife, aren't you? Isn't that you? Oh, I see. You've come for his share, is that it? That's what you want? His share?"

Binty started to answer, but I interrupted her.

"You didn't kill him, Helen. He's not dead."

She turned to me. Her eyes, I noticed, were a split-second slower than her head. The mouth opened, the laughter came again, but her face stayed an immobile mask.

"You didn't kill him," I repeated. "Maybe you scared him half to death, but you only winged him. Half of that money's his as I understand it, and if you agree, I'll see to it that he gets it."

She didn't answer. Her mouth was still open, but no sound came out of it. She stared at me dully, uncomprehendingly.

"It's all over, Helen," I said as gently as I could. "Cookie's not coming. Judith. Judith's not coming. She sent us instead. She gave us the money for you. The money in exchange for the painting. We're going to take the painting now. I think it's the best deal you're going to get."

How dumb these words were you'll see in a minute. It was dumb to try to talk to someone who only heard a sentence in a paragraph, dumb to try to speak reason with someone who probably left her full sanity behind when the car she was riding in drove off a New England bridge. The least I could have done was cut out the part about Cookie not coming. Hell, the least I could have done was grab the cannon the minute she let go of it.

Binty came to before I did. She screamed something at me. But as for me, it was like I was hypnotized by that open mouth and the fact that no sound was coming out of it, hypnotized by the reek of turpentine into some deep waking dream where it made perfect sense that things should be happening in slow motion, perfect sense that people should be lighting franc notes with my matches and holding them upside down while they burned into a torch, perfect sense that the whole world should be going up in slow and violent flames. And you could say, if you wanted to, that I'd foreseen what was going to happen and I didn't stop it because somewhere deep down inside I didn't want to. Like in the balls of my feet.

But I'd be the last to be able to tell you you were wrong.

I saw the Professor set fire to the fistful of money. I heard Binty scream. I saw smoke at the base of the easels where the pile of litter and rags was heaviest, purposefully so, and I saw the pile catch in a flaring ring of innocent flames. But there was a gap of time— as short as a split second, as long as your life—when I did nothing. Then the roar went off, inside me as well as outside, a hellish stinking burst of sound, and the adrenalin spurted through my pores, and I lunged out of pure reflex for what was most precious to me.

I didn't get there—a lucky thing too because it would have scorched the skin from my hand. It wasn't the painting, or Binty, or the Professor. Not even the satchel of money. It was the goddamned gun.

But I collided with Helen Raven. We'd charged at cross purposes, but our fantasies flung us forward together, headfirst into the pyre she'd created. One of the easels crashed and the flames soared up at us and past, hot and stinking and delicious. We saw red; we sensed red; all of us, our skin, our bodies, our minds, caught fire in a tremendous enveloping flush of red in all its hues that crushed all sound, heat, smell. Then we staggered out of it, struggling and hurting, and I heard her shriek, a maniacal blend, and my own roar tore out of my burning throat.

I fought with her and lost. She was all strength, a berserk strength magnified a thousandfold by her madness. She tore out of my grasp. She charged the flames again. By this time they'd gone yellow, a solid searing living wall that reached out and devoured her.

I grabbed for her, found hair, neck, and with a terrific wrench flung her backward. She landed on the floor behind me. Her hair and the wool of her jacket were alive with flames. I remember searching frantically for something to beat them with, and my mind must have been shouting: Where are you, Dedini, now that I need you! But the coughing sobs I heard were my own, and all I found finally for Helen Raven was my own smothering body.

They found us there, on the burning floor. I remember that too, vaguely, the sound of their feet on the stairs, like my proverbial horses galloping across the roof of my soul. At some point there was a terrific crack, like the heavens had had enough, but all it was was the skylight exploding outward into the street. By the time the Law arrived, there was nothing much for them to do but drag us out, and when the fire department showed up later in their pointy helmets . . . well, there's always something weirdly attractive about the spectacle of a building with flames shooting out of its head.

I've said I reacted out of reflex, and so had Helen Raven. She'd gone after the fire, Hindu-style, while I, embarrassing as it may be, had gone for the gun.

But so had Binty Dove gone . . . out of pure reflex.

She might have made it too. There must have been confusion on the stairs, and more of it by the time she hit the street. And if Dedini had her on his wanted list, I doubt he'd had time to hand out her description to every one of his spear carriers.

But when she reached the Quai de Jemmapes,

where police vehicles blocked off the cobbled street, with the canal just beyond and the trundle bridges arching across to what would have been freedom, one of the fishermen broke loose from the group on the banks. He was a hell of a fisherman too, with one arm in a sling, and the rod he carried in his good hand had nothing to do with the art of angling. And he shot her dead in the face with it, even as she was running toward him.

EIGHTEEN

IT WAS A BLOODY CONCLUSION, it came in a hurry, and I guess it calls for a tip of the hat of sorts to the Paris Law that they managed to mop up the mess as quickly as they did. In this, though, they had help too. From those high and largely anonymous places, for one, but also from the circumstances themselves. Looked at from this point of view, I only came in at the tail end. Because there's an old French proverb to the effect that if you let things go to wrack and ruin long enough, they'll eventually take care of themselves.

The story the press got, and gave in turn to the jaded masses, was of a modern love triangle. For "modern" read homosexual. According to it, Binty and Helen Raven had been secret lovers, and so intense was their passion that the one had tried to kill the other's husband, and the other had shot and killed her husband's private investigator. The studio—the "clandestine aerie," as it was called—was their love tryst, and it was there that they'd hidden the stolen Blumenstock masterpiece. How the fire had started no one knew. Some said a lover's quarrel, others an accident. But their passion had gone up in flames along with a great work of art, and it was there, on the smoke-scarred quay, that the husband, maddened by jealousy, had taken his revenge. Such minor discrepancies like what the Law was doing there ahead of time, or why they'd stolen the great work of art, or why said great work of art had once been called a fake, got buried in the lurid details, and when you put together sex, fire, murder, art, plus the fact that the three principals were Americans . . . well, you can imagine what it did for circulation.

Farfetched? Sure it was farfetched. We live, friend, in a farfetched era.

More to the point: would it hold together?

At first glance you wouldn't think so. After all, there were too many people involved; besides, weren't we always taught in Sunday school that the truth will out? But once you start going down the list of those who really knew enough to make waves . . .

Take a closer look, in alphabetical order:

ALAN DOVE. He was the one with the most to lose, and the least. If they'd wanted to, the Law could have laid three murders in his lap, plus fraud, plus receipt and sale of stolen property, plus unpaid bills, bad checks, plus anything else they happened to have lying around. In other words, he was in a pretty mediocre bargaining position. Actually, I doubt he even tried for once, and this because, to the French mentality, the

crime passionnel is the most understandable and therefore condonable of crimes, the more so when the crim-
inal is an enraged husband. He might do time—justice
must after all be served—but he'd do it far from the
rock pile and further from the guillotine.

BINTY DOVE. The dead, like they say, tell no
stories.

J.-C. FLEURIE. Limited knowledge. Things down
at Exceptional Detective may have been on the turbu-
lent side for a while, what with nosy reporters, but
there are times when one has no choice but to cooperate with the authorities.

BERNARD LASCAULT. Everything to gain by the
story as published. Business as usual at Arts Mondiaux, and his American connection intact. How his
new partnership might work out, only time would tell,
but we all have to learn the hard way.

COOKIE LASCAULT. The loss of the Blumenstock compensated for by the two Rillington-
Blumenstocks. Of course her 160,000 francs had gone
up in smoke too, but presumably she could afford it.
At least if she put in an insurance claim, nobody's ever
asked me for my testimony.

HELEN RAVEN. A potential threat, even a serious
one. But it would be a long time before the Professor
could talk to anybody about anything, and then probably only her psychiatrist could make sense of it. Said
psychiatrist, to be sure, would operate a sanatorium a
long way from Paris, and the bills would be paid, as
long as necessary, by an unknown benefactor.

WILLIAM RILLINGTON. Picked up by the Law,
then disappeared. Conceivably the grant-in-aid he had

been receiving from Al Dove has been taken up by another source, and it wouldn't be surprising to see such a promising star emerge in the art constellations of the future.

SUSAN SMITH. Limited knowledge. Subsequently disappeared, as did all Alan Dove's former employees.

JOHNNY VEE. Left the country, along with those of his friends who had been picked up by the Law. Presumed alive and well in California. No reason, for the moment, to meddle further with his French investment.

There are, of course, at least three significant omissions from this list. Messieurs les Commissaires, to mention two. But the Service de la Répression des Fraudes Artistiques could now finally close the dossier on Alan Dove, *courtier en tableaux,* and go on to more important matters, like all those people copying the Mona Lisa in the Louvre. Whereas the Police Judiciaire . . . ? Well, they had their case all right, open and shut, complete with accused and murder weapon, and besides, do you think you could spend twenty-eight years in the service and not know who's going to sign your pension checks?

Which leaves just one.

They took me and Helen Raven away in an ambulance. She was in shock and she'd been burned badly, and the skin-graft boys at the hospital were going to have a hell of a time figuring out how to make some semblance of a human being out of her. Me, I'd just been burned. It was mostly my hands and arms, and superficially, and the treatment I got wasn't much more elaborate than what I could have done myself with a lump of cow's butter. Still, they kept me there some thirty-six hours, and either the no-visitors sign was up or my friends and relatives, wherever they are, had given up the ghost. Finally, after they'd taken my temperature early Tuesday morning, I got out of bed, managed to put my clothes on, and simply walked out of the joint, and nobody so much as checked me to see if I was making off with the Demerol.

It was passing weird, to be standing on a Paris street in the morning, alone and anonymous, with nobody to chase me and nobody to chase. The weather had changed too. It was unseasonably cold, a weak drizzle was falling, and from the gray look of the sky, it would get thicker before it got thinner.

I had a passing notion to head for the apartment in Montparnasse. The wind was blowing, though it was the wrong wind, and so were the trees wrong, but together they made Montparnasse seem a long way off. I found a cab in the taxi rank outside the hospital and rode to the hotel instead.

The Giulia was parked in the street, with two tickets stuck under the windshield wipers. I paid the taxi and went inside. The desk clerk handed me my key and a stack of messages, but he paid me no more mind than if I'd just gone out to buy a newspaper.

I went upstairs to my suite.

Most of the messages were from Freddy Schwartz, and no sooner had I opened the door than the phone started to ring. It was a collect call, from California, would I accept the charges? Yes I would, and gladly. I must have needed the sound of a familiar voice.

Freddy Schwartz was full of booze and disclosure. He was also very pissed off. He'd been trying to get me for three days. Where the fuck had I been for three days?

"I've been around, Fred," I said, but my own voice sounded peculiar to me.

"*Around?* Well for Christ's sake . . . !"

"Never mind," I said. "Give me what you've got."

He did too, and listening, I could almost believe that what had happened had been a bad dream, and that the bandages on my hands were part of it, and that when I hung up I could go back into the bedroom and talk some more about what the B. F. stood for. Well, almost. Because what he had was the following: 1) that Binty Dove had indeed gotten to Paris before Al Dove's soirée; 2) that Bernard Lascault had been in L.A. the week before and had only gone back Saturday; 3) that when he'd gone back, he'd taken some company along, including Johnny Vee; 4) . . .

Well, I forget what 4) was.

"Hell, Cagey," said Freddy Schwartz, "you remember Johnny Vee, don't you?"

"Yes, I remember Johnny Vee."

"Well . . . ? Christ Almighty, you're really onto something all right! You've got them by the short hairs, Cagey! Right by the balls!"

"I know, Freddy. Right by the balls."

"Well . . . ?"

"Nothing. I'm just trying to figure out what to do next."

"*What to do?* Well for Christ's sake, Johnny Vee, that's the big time, Cagey, that's dangerous company!"

"I know, Fred. Only . . ."

"Only what?"

But I wasn't up to telling him. Instead I thanked him for his good work. He sounded somehow disappointed. He told me to be good, and careful if I couldn't be good. I said I'd be good and careful. He told me to let him know how it came out. I said I would. He asked me, plaintively kind of, if when it was all over I wouldn't be coming home for a while? I said I didn't know, but that if I did we'd split a bottle of Four Roses together.

"V.O.," he said, chuckling hoarsely.

"V.O.," I agreed.

I hung up and stared down at my hands. I had it in mind to strip the bandages off. But just then the phone rang again.

It was the desk clerk.

"There are two gentlemen to see you, Monsieur."

"Tell them to wait five minutes, then send them up."

"I'm sorry, Monsieur. They're already in the elevator."

A minute later they came charging in, huffing and puffing and pissed as hell that I'd checked out of the hospital without telling them.

In spite of its name, the Charles de Gaulle Airport at

Roissy is the French answer to *2001*. Maybe Notre Dame's only twenty kilometers away like they say, but you still get the feeling that everything's been flown in from somewhere else, not only the people, and that the voices announcing the flights are really tapes of human beings made a thousand years ago. What with my Air France connection, I'd come to know my way around pretty well, but when I went looking for the men's room on one of those rolling rugs, I still never knew for sure that I wasn't going to end up on the shuttle run to Mars till I heard the flush.

In any case, that was where I ended up that dismal Tuesday, against my will, in a small low-ceilinged office sandwiched on an intermediate level between Arrivals and Departures and belonging to something called the Frontier Air Police. My two escorts had brought me there. They didn't know anything about Dedini or his bargain. Neither did the Frontier Air Police. All the escorts knew was that they were to deliver me to the Frontier Air Police with baggage and passport, and all the Frontier Air Police knew was that I was ticketed for Air France's one o'clock flight, destination New York. Only there was some kind of complication, nobody knew what. And so they left me there, with an armed guard on the other side of the door, and I did my slow-burn routine, and stripped the bandages off my hands.

I remember I was flexing and counting my fingers— there were ten of them, and they seemed to work all right—when Dedini walked in the door.

He'd dressed for the occasion, meaning that he had on the same baggy gray suit but also a little ribbon stuck in the buttonhole of his lapel. Probably it had to do with what he'd done during the war. I didn't ask. His jaw was set, square and heavy, and when the Frontier Air Police functionary started to follow him in, he told him to fuck off, politely but firmly.

He was carrying one of those cardboard dossiers that ties with a strap. He sat down behind the empty desk in the office, put the dossier down in front of him, took out his rimless glasses, adjusted them to his nose, unbuckled the dossier. Only then did he look at me.

"*Eh bien, Monsieur Cage,*" he said. "*Voilà.*"

He handed across a sheaf of papers. Actually there were three sets, each several sheets long, and each held together by a small ring with a red ribbon tied through it. I flipped through them. The second two were copies of the first, and the signature places on the last pages were blank. I turned back to the original and read it through, slowly and carefully.

It was a clever piece of work. By itself it wouldn't have made all that much sense, but if you knew the events as they'd happened, you could guess the official version this "deposition" would go to support. There were few outright lies in it. The Lascaults were never mentioned. As for me, I was just an old friend of the Doves.

Clever, like I say.

I looked at Dedini. He looked at me.

"Suppose I don't sign it," I said.

"If you don't sign it, Monsieur," he answered, "you'll be in New York at three o'clock, I believe. Local time."

I hesitated. Then:

"You offered me a deal, Monsieur le Commissaire. Maybe you'd like to forget it, but I haven't. I delivered them all to you: the Doves, Helen Raven, even Rillington. Now you're welching on your deal."

His jaws tightened, and the scum expression came back strongly. What he said is hard to translate, but it was the only time he let his hair down with me, and I'll give it a try.

"You son of a bitch," he said. "If it wasn't for me, my intervention, they'd have had you on the first flight out yesterday morning. If . . ."

I got the feeling he had a lot more to add, maybe twenty-eight years' worth, but he caught himself, broke it off. He removed his glasses, wiped them, put them back on. Twenty-eight years of service. He glanced at his watch.

"It's the same to me whatever you do, Monsieur. You have five minutes to make your choice."

In fact, it didn't take me that long. The images came and went in a hurry. Al Dove and Binty were in them, and Johnny Vee, and surfers catching a big wave off Newport, and Freddy Schwartz sopping up his sauce, and palm trees and golfers, and the smog backing up against the hills behind Santa Anita. All these on the one hand. And on the other? The stale smell of Gauloises, the sour fruity taste of white wine, traffic jams and Bernard Lascault, the rain dripping on the eaves in Montparnasse, that special feel of French scruff rubbing against your leg. The past vs. the present. "Purity," American-style, vs. a certain kind of built-in corruption that must go back as far as Charlemagne. What was it some Frenchman had said to me? *The only difference between us, Monsieur, is that you wash your hands after you urinate, and I before.*

"You got a coin, Monsieur le Commissaire?"

"What's that?" he said, creasing his eyebrows.

"Never mind," I answered. "It's just that I'm tired of making choices."

I fished in my pockets and came up with one of those precious twenty-centime pieces. I examined it. One side was the profiled bust of a dame with "*République*" running up her nose and "*Française*" down her hair. The back side had the number "20" on it and up above, a little off-center, "*Liberté Egalité Fraternité.*"

"The lady says I stay, the number says I go."

I flipped it in the air, and it landed on the desk.